Jennifer Says Good·bye

by Jane Sorenson

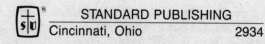

STANDARD PUBLISHING
Cincinnati, Ohio   2934

Library of Congress Cataloging in Publication Data

Sorenson, Jane.
   Jennifer Says Good-bye.

   (A Jennifer book ; 4)
   Summary: After Jennifer's family returns from a visit to her
grandparents in Florida, a death takes them back to Illinois for the
first time since their move to Pennsylvania.

   [1. Death—Fiction.   2. Christian life—Fiction]   I. Title.
II. Series: Sorenson, Jane. Jennifer book ; 4.
PZ7.S7214Je   1984   [Fic]   84-218
ISBN 0-87239-774-2

To Mel
For sharing Jennifer's laughter and tears

1

Time to Think

Lord, it's me, Jennifer.

I stood near the curb looking for Mom's station wagon. It was my first day not to ride the bus home.

"What's up, Jennifer?" Mack Harrington wondered.

"Dentist appointment," I said.

"See you tomorrow," Mack said. He smiled, turned, and headed toward the bus.

The two girls at the stop acted as if they had never seen me before. But that's not true. I'm in their homeroom, and I live in the same neighborhood. I wonder if Lindsay Porterfield and Stephanie Cantrell will ever like me?

Just then Mom came around the corner. "Hi," she said. "Sorry I'm late."

"What happened?" I asked. I shifted my books into my left hand and pulled the car door shut.

"Nothing," she said. "Am I that late?"

"No," I said. "I mean you look different."

"You don't like my hair."

Well, honesty may be the *best policy,* but sometimes I have my doubts. "Did you try another new place?"

"You guessed," Mom said. "I don't know whether to laugh or cry."

I was glad I hadn't picked honesty.

"This guy was called Mr. Chaz. King of Prussia."

"Are you still looking in the Yellow Pages?" I asked.

"Well, it sounded good," Mom said. She pulled out into the traffic.

Frankly I'm glad I've been letting my hair grow.

"I used to laugh at people who moved away and came back for their permanents," Mom said.

"You aren't thinking of flying to Illinois?" I said. But actually it sounded kind of neat.

"Well," Mom said, "maybe we could fly Judy to Philadelphia. If I don't find someone who can cut my hair right, how will I ever get a permanent?"

"Have you considered asking Mrs. Harrington?" I glanced at Mom.

"Yes, but I hate having to ask her *everything.*"

"I'm sure she doesn't mind," I said. "After all, Pete and Mike are best friends. And," I added, "Mack and Matthew are in my school."

"I know," Mom said. She looked at me out of the

corner of her eye. I saw her! Then she concentrated on driving.

"Didn't you meet women at that coffee last week?" I asked.

"Yes, and everyone was lovely and polite. But Martha Harrington is the only neighbor who has come over."

It isn't as if I don't understand *the problem*. Our neighborhood just isn't what you'd call *close*. In my own case, now I have the girls at church. And I'm meeting kids at school.

"Hey, Mom," I said quickly. "I've got an idea. How about if I ask one of the girls?"

Mom didn't say anything. She turned into the drive next to the dentist's office.

"I'll say I'm considering getting my hair cut," I continued. "Which isn't exactly a lie." All of a sudden I got a brainstorm. "Chris!" I said. "If any woman would know a good stylist, it would be Mrs. McKenna!"

Mom looked alert as she parked the car. "I think you're right," she said. There was almost a lilt in her voice. "When is your next riding lesson?"

"Tomorrow," I said. "But I can call her tonight."

"Thanks," Mom said. "Jennifer," she added, "please don't tell her how desperate I am. OK?"

"I won't." I smiled. "Are you going to wait for me?"

"No. I have to pick up a few things at Super Saver. Will you be long?"

I shrugged my shoulders. "Your guess is good. Can I leave my books in the car?"

I was halfway up the stairs when I realized my goof. How stupid can I be? I had completely forgotten that Dr. Crawford doesn't have any good magazines.

So I had to sit in her waiting room and *think*. First I thought about which Harrington boy I liked best, Matthew or Mack? No decision. Next, I thought about You, Lord. As You know. I thought about how neat youth group and Sunday school are. And that reminded me of my Sunday-school class in Illinois.

I started wondering what would have happened if my father hadn't been promoted. What if we hadn't moved to Philadelphia in June? But we did. And, as the saying goes, the rest is *history.*

"Jennifer." It was the nurse.

I looked up and headed into Dr. Crawford's clutches. I only hoped she'd be more gentle today. But by the time I was done, I was almost in tears. And I still didn't have the nerve to tell my parents about my new orthodontist.

Mom was sitting in the car reading a paperback. "Don't ever let me forget to take something to read," I said. "Her only magazines are comic books and sports."

"So, why not read about sports?"

I couldn't believe it. "I'm not interested in *reading* about sports," I said. It really didn't matter anyway. We were turning into our subdivision. "What's for supper?"

"That Japanese hamburger recipe."

I smiled. Pete and Justin can't stand it, but it's one of my favorites.

As we entered the study, I could hear my brothers yelling. They were beating each other up—just like they used to do in Illinois.

"Take it back," Justin was hollering.

"I won't. It's the truth, and you know it!"

"Mom's here, and I'll tell."

"Go ahead, Tattletale. You know it's true." There was a pause. "Justin's got a girl friend!"

Mom set her groceries on the counter. "Hey, that's enough, guys." Naturally they didn't pay any attention.

"Tell me her name, and I'll stop."

"You creep," Justin yelled. "You'd never have gotten me down if you hadn't caught me by surprise."

"What's her name?" Pete shouted.

"Nicole," Justin said. "But she's not my girl friend."

Mom and I stood there watching. Pete released Justin, who wiggled free and stood up with dignity. It's hard to have dignity when you're as small as Justin, but he pulled it off. "You're just jealous anyway," he said. And, from the look on Pete's face, Justin could have been *right*.

At that point we heard the garage door going up, and Dad walked in. He was wearing his silly grin. The one he wears when something is *going to happen*.

Even Mom looked puzzled. "What's up?" she asked.

"I'll tell you at dinner," he said. "What are we having?"

"That nice Japanese hamburger."

"Oh," said Dad. He tossed his briefcase on the desk. And then he grinned again.

2

Spring's a Little Late

Lord, it's me, Jennifer.

Well, as You know, Justin slipped into his chair just in the nick of time before Dad called on him to pray. We all sat there.

But, instead of reciting our family's standard prayer, he began an original version. "Lord," he said, "even though this isn't my favorite meal, thanks anyhow. And please get Pete off my back. Amen."

It was the first time I've ever heard him pray like that. And, frankly, it left the family more than a little upset.

"You might call that praying," Pete said. "I consider it religious tattling!"

Mom wasn't happy either. "If you have complaints

about the food, you can take it up with the cook," she said. "No need to go to the Management."

I glanced at Dad. Did I catch a glimmer of a smile? Personally, not considering the contents, I thought it was pretty neat that Justin had the courage to talk to You in front of the whole family. But what do I know?

"Is this really served in Japan?" Pete asked.

"How should I know?" Mom said. "It's just a recipe. Could you please eat it before it gets cold?"

"I agree," said Dad. He took a bite and pretended to savor the taste. Even Mom had to smile. Besides, we all knew that Dad was going to make an announcement. It was just a matter of time.

He stalled as long as he could. He's always been a little dramatic. "How was school today?" Nobody said anything. "Didn't any of you go to school today?" We all giggled.

I decided it was an open invitation to do a little bragging. "I got an A on my English paper."

"That's great," said Dad. "Make way for Jennifer Green, journalist."

I felt good.

"You look happy, Justin," Dad said. "Anything special?" As You know, Lord, only two weeks ago he was crying at school every day. Naturally, Dad didn't bring that up.

"I'm on the soccer team for our class," Justin said.

"And," said Pete before anyone else could comment, "he has a girl friend."

"My prayer wasn't answered," Justin said.

"That will do, Pete," Mom said. "It's bad enough that you should beat each other up over it. No need to spoil dinner besides." Pete looked at his plate.

"What's new in your life, Pete?" Dad asked his older son.

"Not much," he replied. "Not much at all." He acted sort of limp. I looked straight at him, but he kept his eyes on his plate. Everybody could tell he had *troubles*. The amazing thing is that Pete's the one in the family that made the fastest and happiest adjustment when we moved.

"Well," Dad said, "I was going to wait until dessert to surprise you, but I just can't keep the secret. How many of you would like to join me on a trip?" He reached into his pocket and pulled out a folder of airline tickets.

"Wow," said Justin.

"Where are we going?" I asked. "Illinois?" We haven't been back since we moved.

"Not this time," Dad said. "Guess again."

Well, to be honest, I was stumped. We've never gone anywhere before. Except to visit Grandma and Grandpa Green in Florida during spring vacation. And this wasn't spring or even vacation.

Mom didn't know either. I could tell. But she was getting excited too. "Florida?" she guessed.

Dad grinned like a ninny. "You've got it!" he announced.

"You're kidding," Pete said.

"No, I'm not," Dad replied. "Remember when we couldn't go down last spring?"

Of course everybody remembered. It was one of the worst announcements of our life.

"Those meetings I had to attend last spring resulted in my promotion to East Coast Vice President," Dad reminded us.

"And we ran the furniture store so Aunt Carol and Uncle Bob and Sarah and Michael could go to Florida instead," I said.

"You were such good sports," Dad said. "I was so proud of you all."

"And then we moved," I said. "It seems like a lot longer than a few months, doesn't it?"

"A year or two, at least," Mom agreed.

"Well," Dad said, "I think we all deserve a vacation. And Grandma and Pops can hardly wait to see you." He handed Mom the tickets.

"So soon!" Mom said. "Why, that's only a few days away."

"I checked it out," Dad said. "It's the week of Teachers' Institute and Parent Conferences. You won't miss much school."

I couldn't believe my ears. Always before, we had to have a temperature even to miss gym! Has Dad stopped being *strict?*

"Naturally, I'll expect you to make up your work before we go. You can get your assignments tomorrow," Dad said.

"I guess I'll just have to miss soccer," Justin realized.

That got me to thinking. I'll miss my riding lessons. And we will miss Sunday school and church. Plus, I'll miss youth group.

"Mike and I were going to our last Phillies game," Pete said.

"Isn't it wonderful," Mom said, "you're involved enough here already to have things to miss!" I realized that she wouldn't miss anything—except grocery shopping. I feel sad for her.

"But is everybody going to Florida?" Dad asked. We all cheered. "I've rented a three-bedroom condo in my parents' building for next week. It just became available," Dad explained.

"Won't we be with Grandma and Pops?" Pete asked.

"Of course," Dad said. "We'll go places, fish, all the usual stuff. But this will give us more bedrooms. I think we'll all sleep better."

"How about meals?" Justin asked. Eating is one of our favorite things. Grandma Green is a super cook. She fixes anything we want to eat. Or else we eat out in restaurants.

"As usual," Dad said. "Everything the same as usual."

I don't know when I've felt so happy, Lord. When our grandparents were running the furniture store in our hometown, it was so neat. I guess nobody ever had greater grandparents than we have. When they retired to Florida, it left a hole in our lives. Of course, we still had

14

Mom's parents. Now we don't have anybody who has known us all our lives. Not in Philadelphia.

After dinner, I rushed to the phone to call Chris. She's my riding instructor and also my friend. I had promised to check on hair stylists for Mom, and I didn't want to forget.

"Mom's drunk," Chris stated bluntly. "But I'll try to ask her in the morning before I go to school."

"Thanks," I said. "I have something exciting to tell you. See you after school."

I passed Justin in the upstairs hall. "Hi," I said. "What's with Pete?" "I don't know," he said. "He acted funny after school. And when Nicole sat down next to me on the bus, he made it into a *big deal*."

"Was it?" I wondered.

"Well," said Justin, "I guess maybe it was." He disappeared into his room.

3

Bus Stop

Lord, it's me, Jennifer.

I can definitely tell fall is here. For one thing, the mornings are getting darker. Although getting up is harder, getting dressed is easier. There's less chance that if I wear jeans or a wool skirt I might be sweating by lunch.

On the way out of my room, I grabbed my light blue cardigan and my books. My homework was in a neat stack. It is called *being organized*. Somehow I guess I learned it from my mother.

It was an *oatmeal day*. "Oh, no," I muttered, as I sat down at the kitchen table.

"That's enough, Jennifer," Mom said. "I expect you to be a good example to your brothers."

"They aren't here. And you know I hate oatmeal," I said.

"Try brown sugar on it," Mom suggested.

"It doesn't help."

"You haven't tried it yet," Mom said.

"Well, maybe not today. But you pull that line with me every time we have oatmeal. Can't you think of something else?"

"You should be glad I care enough to get up and fix your breakfast," Mom said. "Plenty of mothers don't."

She had a *point*. It was one of those times when, looking back, you wonder how it started. It really wasn't worth it, but somehow nobody would give in. I ate in silence.

"Good morning, Pete," Mom said. I looked up as my brother sat down.

"Hi," Pete said. "Can I go to Mike's after school?"

"OK," Mom said. "I have to take Jennifer to Twin Pines for her lesson. She has to change to her riding jeans. Be sure you change your pants." She looked up and paused. "Oh, my goodness."

There on the steps to our eating area stood Justin. He looked like an ad for the Sears Back-to-School catalog. Yellow Izod sweater, navy cords, new Nikes.

"You used a blower on your hair," Pete accused.

Justin slid into his chair and attacked the bowl of oatmeal Mom had just dished up. "So what if I did?"

"Did you leave any hot water?" Pete caught my eye.

"Don't ever take a shower after Justin!" he warned.

"Did you use my blow dryer?" I asked.

No answer. Justin kept eating.

"Hey," I said. "Did you?"

"It was just sitting there. How do I look?"

"Next time, ask," I said. "It looks good."

I glanced at my watch. "Oh, no," I said. "I'm late."

"You just want to get there early so you can talk to Matthew. Or is it Mack?" Pete asked.

"A lot you know," I replied.

Mom poured herself a cup of coffee. She thinks mornings are her worst time of the day. Frankly I wouldn't know.

It was more peaceful as I walked down our lane. The trees are getting beautiful. All the dogwoods that were in bloom last spring now are wearing red leaves and berries. Most of the taller trees are still green. I turned left at our mailbox and headed for the junior high bus stop. Both Matthew and Mack were already waiting. "Hi," I said to both of them. "Guess what?"

"You've just won second prize in a beauty contest," said Matthew. He's in ninth grade. We're both on Student Council.

"Nope," I said. "Our family is going to Florida at the end of the week."

"No kidding!" Mack sounded impressed. He sits behind me in homeroom. "What's the occasion?"

"Dad's parents retired down there several years ago. They have a condo right on the water."

"Lucky you!" said Matthew.

"We usually go during spring vacation, but this year we couldn't. It's a long story. Anyhow, Dad has plane tickets for Friday night," I said. "I'm going to have to work like mad to make up my homework by then." I was so excited I didn't even notice Lindsay and Stephanie walk up.

"Well, hi, Jennifer," Lindsay said. The only time they talk to me is when I'm with the Harrington boys.

"Hi," I said.

"Are you Justin Green's sister?" she asked.

"Well, sure," I said. It's the first time anybody has ever asked me that. To be honest, I usually think of him as my brother!

"My sister thinks he's darling!" Lindsay gushed.

I couldn't think of anything to say. So I just stood there. Finally I asked, "Is your sister named Nicole?"

"Right on," Lindsay smiled. "You mean he's actually mentioned her at home?"

I felt as if I had betrayed Justin. "Well," I said, "he's mentioned quite a few girls."

Matthew grinned. The Harringtons take us to church, so naturally they know my brothers.

"It's a small world, isn't it?" said Stephanie, not wanting to be left out. "In my case, my sister is in Mark Harrington's class. I'm sure you've heard of Ashlie."

Matthew kept a serious face. "Ashlie who?"

"Oh, you big tease!" Stephanie pretended to be upset. What a fake!

"Yes," agreed Lindsay. "Boys are all alike."

19

"Maybe in your opinion," I said. "Personally, I don't agree." Usually I think of good comebacks about two days later. I decided this was going to be a good day.

The bus pulled up. As the Harrington brothers headed for the back of the bus, I slipped into my usual seat. Heidi Stoltzfus from my Sunday-school class gets on later and usually joins me.

"Jennifer," Stephanie said. I couldn't believe it. Once the guys are gone, they always act as if I don't exist.

I turned around. "Yes?" I said.

"Would you like to go trail riding with us tomorrow afternoon?"

I couldn't believe my ears. I tried to act cool. "It sounds like fun," I said. "But since I moved here I haven't gotten my own horse yet." I hope that didn't sound like a total lie. The truth was, in Illinois I never even touched a horse, much less owned one!

"I'm sure you can ride my sister's," Stephanie said.

"Well," I said, "I'll have to check my schedule. We're going out of town the end of the week."

"Call me tonight," Stephanie said. She wrote a number on a sheet of notebook paper and tore it off. "We have an unlisted number," she explained.

"Hope you can make it," Lindsay added. She watched as Heidi got on the bus.

"Hi, Jennifer," Heidi said. "You look happy! What's new?"

"We're going to Florida to visit our grandparents in a few days." The more I said it, the more excited I got.

"You mean you're getting off school?"

"Uh huh." I grabbed my books as we turned a corner. "We haven't seen them in over a year—partly because of our moving."

"I'm glad I live close to my grandparents. It must be hard to give that up. Of course, some kids never know what it's like." Heidi is the most understanding girl I know in Pennsylvania.

Then I had a thought. "Can I ask you something, Heidi?"

"Sure," she said. "Anything you want to know." She smiled. "Except about fashions!" We both laughed. Most of the kids are really into the latest fads. I think it started with designer jeans. Heidi doesn't even own any jeans. That tells you something.

I lowered my voice. "I think my grandparents are Christians," I whispered. This is very exciting, because I just became one myself at a retreat. As You know, Lord!

"That's great," Heidi said.

"Well, how can I know for sure?" I wondered.

"Listen for clues when they talk," Heidi said. "You must have some clues already, since you think they are."

"They pray in restaurants," I said.

"Sounds suspicious," Heidi said. We both laughed again. "Of course, you could tell them about the retreat and see what they say."

"Why didn't I think of that?"

The bus parked and everybody headed for the school. Another day began.

4

Things Are Changing

Lord, it's me, Jennifer.

"I thought those girls didn't even speak to you," Chris said. She and I usually talk after my riding lesson.

"They didn't," I said. "Except when Matthew and Mack were around."

"Then how come they want you to go riding?"

"I don't know. Maybe they've changed," I answered.

"Do you really think so?"

"Well, it does seem funny. Maybe it's because Lindsay's sister has a crush on Justin. Did I tell you he used my blow dryer this morning?"

"No kidding!" Chris started laughing. "She must really be something."

"I don't know her. Lindsay is pretty. Tall and blond." I hate to admit it, but it's the truth.

"What's her last name?" Chris asked.

"Porterfield."

"Oh, we know them. They're members at one of the clubs. The younger sister is boy crazy. Better warn Justin."

"He's just a kid," I said. "And you know how small he is."

"Well, little sister looks and acts twice her age. Take it from me."

I changed the subject. "Tell me the truth, Chris. Do you think I ride well enough to go with them?" I asked.

"Sure. You ride better than a lot of kids who've taken lessons for years. And, after all, trail riding isn't an international competition."

"Thanks, Chris," I said. "You're a super teacher. It's just that I don't want to make a fool of myself."

"In other words, you want to impress them." She has an annoying way of getting to the point.

"Of course not," I denied.

"Are you trying to get into their crowd?" Chris continued. "Believe me, it isn't worth it."

"I don't have any girl friends in our neighborhood," I admitted.

"Then why didn't you say so?"

"I thought I did. Hey, Chris," I said, "thanks for checking on the hair stylist for Mom. She'll be happy for a recommendation. She really likes you."

"Well, my mom's gone to that shop for years. How they put up with her I really don't know. If you know what I mean."

I know. Chris' mother is a beautiful woman. But she drinks a lot.

Just as we walked out of the stable, Mom drove up. "Oh, no," I said, "I didn't have a chance to tell you we're going to Florida to see our grandparents. We leave on Friday. So I'll miss my lessons."

"How long will you be gone?"

"About a week." I glanced at Mom waiting in the car. "It's really unusual—for us to go this time of the year, I mean. We didn't get to go in the spring, and then we moved. Did I tell you about my grandparents?"

Chris shook her head.

"They really are special," I said. But Mom was looking impatient. "I guess I'd better go. I'll tell you all about them when I get back."

"Promise?"

"Promise!" I said.

"Hey, have a great time," she called as we left.

"Hi," I greeted Mom. "I have the name of a hair stylist." I fished around in my jeans pocket. "Here." I handed the name to Mom.

"Thanks. I wonder if they can take me before we leave? A good cut would give me a real lift right now."

"You still mad about the oatmeal?" I asked.

"Of course not," Mom said. "I think I'm just tired. A week in Florida sounds wonderful, doesn't it?"

"I'm planning to go trail riding tomorrow with Lindsay and Stephanie," I said. "Mrs. Cantrell will drive us. And I can ride an older sister's horse." Mom kept driving. "Did I tell you Lindsay's younger sister is Nicole—Justin's friend?"

"I'm trying to keep everybody straight," Mom said.

After supper, which was surprisingly calm after last night, I decided to call Stephanie. I nearly panicked when I couldn't find her number. But it was right where I left it.

"This is Stephanie Cantrell," she said. Her voice was cool and sort of low and gentle.

My voice sounded bouncy and immature. But I didn't have time to change it. She was waiting on the other end of the line. "This is Jennifer Green," I said.

"Well, hi, Jennifer!" I couldn't believe it. I had halfway expected her not to remember who I was.

"I called to tell you I can go trail riding tomorrow afternoon," I said. That was right to the *point*. Maybe too much so.

"That's wonderful," Stephanie said. "Why don't you bring your riding clothes to school, and we can all change at the stable. Mom will pick us up to save time."

"Are you sure it's OK with your sister if I ride her horse?" I asked. I felt a little uncomfortable about it.

"No problem," Stephanie insisted. "She'll be happy to have him exercised. She really doesn't have enough time for a horse any more. Did I tell you she's a senior?"

"I figured she must be, since she knows Mark Harrington," I said.

"How do you know the Harringtons?" Stephanie asked. "I've been wondering since school started."

"From church," I said. I decided not to tell her they give us a ride. My parents usually don't go.

"Oh, that's it," said Stephanie. "I've got to go now. See you tomorrow."

Later, after my homework was done, I stuck my riding boots in a shopping bag with some old riding jeans and a sweat shirt. I wondered what I was getting into. There was a light knock on my door.

"Hi, Justin! Come on in," I said, gently closing the door. "How are things?"

He's started to smile a lot. "When you were my age, did you like a boy?" he asked.

I tried to think. Not that it was so hard. I've always secretly liked somebody or other. "Yes," I said.

"Did you tell him?"

"No way!" I said.

"I guess things are changing," Justin said.

"So, did you hear that on television?" I asked. Honestly!

"Nope."

"Then why are you asking?" But I started getting a funny feeling.

"Nicole told me." He looked sort of embarrassed.

"Well," I said, "she probably likes a lot of boys."

"Not like me."

"How do you know?"

"She invited me to watch a movie with her on their VCR Saturday."

"Of course, you can't go," I said.

"Why not?" He seemed irritated.

I realized how much my voice sounded like Mom's. I had to back off. "We're going to Florida on Friday night. Remember?"

"Of course I know we're going. But when she asked me, I forgot." Was it my imagination, or did he seem relieved?

"I'm really excited about going!" I said.

"I am too," Justin agreed. "Pops is one of my favorite people in the whole world!"

"I guess we all agree on that."

"Hey, thanks, Jennifer," he said, turning toward the door.

"It was nothing," I said modestly. But after he left I realized that the problem isn't gone, only delayed. Good grief, Lord, things really are changing!

5

Pride
Goeth Before

Lord, it's me, Jennifer.

I guess I should have known I was in trouble when I saw Stephanie and Lindsay get on the bus. Each carried a beautiful sports tote bag. One navy with burgundy trim, the other all burgundy.

I glanced down at my paper shopping bag and felt ashamed.

"Hi, Jennifer," Lindsay said, as they passed my seat.

"Hi," I said, hoping they hadn't looked on the floor between my feet.

"It's a perfect day for a ride," said Stephanie, as they sat down behind me.

She was right. It was a beautiful day.

It seemed like an eternity until Heidi got on. I tried to think of my options. It was too late to be needed at home. I might "get sick," but if I didn't recover fast, I'd mess up Florida and getting my homework done.

"Hi," Heidi said. "Are you OK?"

I nodded. If I told Heidi the truth, she'd never understand. Not in a million years. Not this. She simply and clearly never worries about what other people think.

"How's Student Council?" she asked.

"Fine," I said. "Naturally I didn't know anyone. But Matthew seems to know everybody, and he's been great at introducing me."

"He's a nice guy," Heidi said. "In fact, the Harringtons are really a great family. When we first started going to the same church, they invited us to dinner."

"You mean you haven't gone there all your life?"

"We lived here. But we changed churches about three years ago," Heidi said.

"I didn't know you could do that," I said.

"It's a free country."

"Well, I know. But why did you change?" This was interesting.

"We got a new minister, and he didn't preach from the Bible," Heidi said.

"What did he preach from?"

"I was pretty young at the time," she said. "But my parents said he didn't believe in Heaven. He thought Jesus was just a great teacher and example to follow—not the Son of God."

I wanted to find out more, but we were at school. "Heidi," I said, "would you help me carry my stuff? I have so many books. Could you manage the shopping bag?"

"No problem," she said as she picked it up.

That shopping bag nearly ruined my day. At first it was all I could think about. But then I stopped thinking about *the bag* and started concentrating on what was inside. Why hadn't I asked for riding pants? I was so busy learning to ride that what I looked like never entered my mind. At least I do have boots.

Maybe I could *fake it!* I wondered if they'd believe I had just outgrown my pants? Or that they were in the wash? Or that somebody had borrowed them? Could they have gotten lost when we moved? I thought of phoning Mom and asking her to buy some and bring them to the principal's office. But I knew she wouldn't. And, with my luck, they wouldn't fit anyhow!

When I finally hit on a *plan,* it was so simple I wondered why I hadn't thought of it in the first place. I just *wouldn't say anything*. I'd act as if riding with them wasn't a big deal. I thought it just might work.

When the last bell rang, I headed for my locker. I took out the books I'd need first, then the brown shopping bag. I put the books inside.

"You going somewhere?" Mack Harrington asked.

"Well," I said, "I have all these books because I have to finish my assignments before we go to Florida. Also," I added, "I'm going trail riding this afternoon."

"It's a beautiful day for it," Mack said. "Can I carry your bag?"

"Why, thank you, Mack," I said.

Stephanie and Lindsay were waiting for me outside. "Mom's over there," Stephanie said.

"Here you go," Mack said, handing me the bag. "Have fun!"

"Thanks again, Mack," I said, smiling. I knew the girls were watching.

If they noticed the bag, nothing was said. We walked over to a beautiful car, and I met Mrs. Cantrell.

"Where did you live before?" Mrs. Cantrell asked me.

"In Illinois. A suburb of Chicago," I said.

"A woman at the club moved to Kenilworth."

"I don't know where that is," I said. So much for the small world routine.

Stephanie's mother turned down a lane and stopped near a barn. "I'll pick you up at five-thirty," she said.

Well, the dressing went fine. I just slipped on my jeans, tucked them into my boots, and didn't say a word. The other girls both put on tan riding pants.

"Ashlie's horse is next to mine," Stephanie said, as she led the way. We stopped by a stall across from Lindsay's. "His name is King."

"Is that the saddle I should use?" I asked.

"Right," Stephanie said. "I'll be next door."

I carefully lifted the saddle into place. I've done it a million times for Rocky. But this saddle was a lot newer. I pulled the girth tight. The hole wasn't large, like on a belt you've worn a lot. I wondered if the stirrups would be the right length. I decided to chance it.

Coming out of the stall, I nearly knocked Lindsay over. "Sorry," I said. I felt really nervous about the stirrups.

I followed Lindsay outside. "I like your horse," I said.

"Thanks," she replied. "Her name's Noel. It's short for Graceful Princess. I got her for Christmas. I'm the only one in my family who rides. Nicole took a few lessons, but she's into volleyball. That's why I keep Noel here with Cantrells' horses."

We both mounted. I can't tell You how relieved I was when the stirrups were OK! I started to relax. Chris was right. She had taught me well, and this wasn't a big deal.

"Finally," said Stephanie, as she came out of the stable. "I didn't think I'd ever get this new saddle on right. Let's go." She led her horse to a gate, opened it, and waited while we rode through.

We walked slowly through a meadow. I couldn't see even one house. The late afternoon sun felt good.

"Hey, follow me," said Stephanie. She went into a slow trot toward a grove of trees. I hung back and let Lindsay go next. It seemed only fair.

For some reason, King lunged forward. I was glad the others couldn't see me. Not cool at all.

Then I felt it. Slowly, gently, I was sliding to the right. What in the world? King had the good sense to stop. By now the saddle had slipped so far that my left knee was on top. I had dropped the reins and was trying to hang onto the cantle for dear life.

Now my own weight pulled the saddle down faster and faster. I didn't have any idea what to do next. So I just tried to hang on. One last slide found the saddle upside down. And I was still in the saddle, underneath the horse, my legs clamped tight.

To say I was scared to death would be an understatement—if You'll pardon the pun. Suddenly I was aware of the sound of the other horses. But at first the girls didn't say anything. And there I hung.

I'm not sure when I started to laugh. Like my descent, it started slowly and built up momentum. I was laughing so hard I could barely hang on. That's how weak I get when I laugh.

And then I heard Lindsay and Stephanie joining in. We were all hysterical. Except my horse. Fortunately, King was so startled he just stood there.

"I've got you," Stephanie said. "Help me, Lindsay. It's OK, Jennifer. You can let go now." But as soon as I was safe, everyone started laughing again.

I didn't know what to say.

Somehow, with the help of the girls, I managed to unfasten the saddle and put it back on top.

"We'd better head back. It's nearly five o'clock," Stephanie said. "I wish I had a camera."

"I can't believe it," I said. "Never in my wildest dreams did I imagine such a thing happening."

"It's funny," Stephanie said, "but when we got the new saddles I wondered what would happen if I didn't get it tight enough."

"Well, now you know," I said. "I hope your sister isn't mad."

"She'll never know," Stephanie promised. "After all, nobody got hurt."

"I think I'll burst out laughing every time I think about it," Lindsay said.

"Can I ask a favor?" I said. "Please don't tell anyone! I don't think I can stand to be the laughingstock of the area. Not now, anyway."

"Well," Lindsay said, "I really don't see much point in telling." But she started laughing again.

We rode back in silence, with an occasional burst of laughter.

I only hope they can be trusted.

6

Pete's Problem

Lord, it's me, Jennifer.

You'd think when you live in the same house with somebody, you'd have lots of time to talk. Wouldn't You?

Then why is it that most of my conversations with my family consist of "When do I have to be home?" "Why can't I go?" Or, in the case of my brothers, jokes and teasing?

Do lots of people spend years eating at the same table and never telling each other how they feel, what they think, or what their dreams are? If I didn't have You to talk to, Lord, life at home would be mostly like a TV talk show—everyone bragging about his most recent honor!

Mom said that once when she had a baby (I can't remember which one of us it was), she told her whole life history to her roommate. And vice versa. And then they never saw each other again!

Dad said sometimes this happens when he flies on airplanes. Which brings me to *my point*. On our trip to Florida, I sat with Pete.

"Are you excited?" I asked.

"Sure," Pete said. "Aren't you?"

"Naturally." But I was also relieved. Dad had come home from the office late, and I was just sure we'd missed the plane. As it was, we had only a few minutes to spare. The plane was full, and standby passengers were waiting to take our seats if we didn't make it.

"When do you think we'll eat?" Pete wondered.

"We haven't even taken off yet," I said. "And then they have to serve drinks. Here," I said, "want some Jujubes?"

A *voice* told us to fasten our seat belts. We already had. As the flight attendant demonstrated what to do in an emergency. I watched carefully. I looked around and realized hardly anyone else was watching. In an emergency, I would have to save the people all by myself! I know You'd help, Lord. But sometimes I get so tired of feeling so responsible.

Pete was busy reading the airline's magazine. It didn't take him long. "Boring," he said, as he tucked it back under the elastic pocket. He tried to look out the window. "I can't see a thing." It was dark outside.

Once I was sure we were safely in the air, I relaxed. I looked across the aisle and one row back to see Dad, plus half of Mom's new haircut, plus none of Justin. He was next to the window. Dad grinned at me. I pretended I hadn't seen him.

"It seems funny leaving from Philadelphia," I said to my brother.

"I was thinking the same thing," Pete said.

"No kidding?" Until now we had always flown to Florida from O'Hare in Chicago.

"Do you miss Illinois?" Pete asked, unfastening his seat belt.

"In some ways," I admitted.

"I can't believe we've been gone such a short time," my brother said.

"I know," I agreed. "Still, I felt as if the summer would never end. At least you had friends."

"I couldn't believe it when those three guys came over the first day," Pete remembered. "I thought I was in Heaven."

"Remember how nervous you were when we were driving to Philadelphia? You were afraid you wouldn't have any friends."

"I was not," Pete said.

I don't know why he had to deny it. I can remember our conversation almost word for word. "Oh, sure," I said. "You mean you can't even remember telling me how scared you were you wouldn't find a friend like Joseph?" I reminded him. He didn't want to be reminded.

"Well," I said, "the Lord was good to give you Mike Harrington and Jeff and Scott. Justin and I didn't have anybody all summer—at least not in the neighborhood."

"You're right, Jennifer," he agreed. "Mike is very special. I think he'll always be my friend."

"How about the others?"

Pete shrugged his shoulders.

"Is something wrong?" I asked.

"No," he answered. Pete stared at the dark window. "Just the usual."

"What do you mean?"

"Oh, nothing. Give me another piece of candy." He took several, and put them all in his mouth at once. I eat them one at a time.

"Look," I said, "you might as well tell me. You've been on cloud nine all summer until this week. And now you look as if you've lost your last friend. So to speak," I added.

"I'm just not coordinated," he said.

"Oh." I waited. Not again, Lord!

"I try so hard. But I feel like Charlie Brown," Pete said softly.

"Sports, I guess," I said. "But Charlie Brown can't help it, and neither can you."

"Tell that to my class!" Pete said. "I'm back to being the last one picked."

I waited. What could be worse?

"We had these stupid tests. We were timed." He looked ashamed.

Suddenly I knew exactly what had happened. "Really bad?" I asked.

"The worst," he admitted. "The absolute worst. Even worse than the girls."

"Hey," I said. "Being a girl doesn't have anything to do with it."

"Try telling that to Jeff Cantrell."

"Ashlie Cantrell's brother?" I said. "You didn't tell me Jeff was Ashlie's brother."

"What difference does it make?"

"None," I agreed. "I was just surprised. I didn't mean to get off the point."

"There isn't anything else to say anyway," Pete said. "It's Illinois all over again. I can't get away from it."

Just then the flight attendant asked us what we wanted to drink. I chose 7-Up and Pete chose Coke. We drank in silence.

"Is that why you picked on Justin the other day?" An ice cube bumped my nose.

"Of course not," Pete said. "He's a *show-off. A hot dog. A jock.*" He paused for effect. "And a dummy."

"Is that all?" I said. "Are you finished? Did you like it better when he was crying every day?"

Pete looked embarrassed. "I stuck by him then."

"Mighty wonderful of you." I gave up on my drink. "The poor little kid didn't have a friend in the world, and his big brother stuck by him. Big deal!"

"Just get off my case," Pete said. "I don't know why I thought you would understand."

He was right. He was hurting, and I just kicked him. Some big sister you are Jennifer Green! "I'm sorry. Please forgive me."

Pete looked surprised. I wonder if that's the first time I ever asked him to forgive me. Is it, Lord?

"Well, OK," he said.

"Are you sure?" I don't want any hard feelings between us.

"I know how to forgive," Pete said. He had a funny look on his face. I didn't know whether to ask him what he meant or not. But just then our dinners came.

"What do you think that is?" Pete said, pointing to the mystery meat.

"Beats me," I said. "Taste it."

"You first." He was laughing. "I'm too young to die."

"I think it's beef," I said. "But I wouldn't stake my life on it."

"You mean 'steak' your life on it?" Pete was laughing at his own joke.

I glanced around at Dad. He was grinning at me. And at the back of Pete's seat.

Suddenly I thought I heard Justin's voice saying, "Yuck!" It might have been my imagination. But I don't think so.

7

Our Arrival

Lord, it's me, Jennifer.

We were landing. The No Smoking sign was on, and we were being told to fasten our seat belts. In spite of the time, I was wide awake, and so was Pete. I wondered about Justin.

"Flying is like magic," Pete said. "Suddenly you are in a new place. Driving is so gradual."

I remembered our trip to Philadelphia when we moved. We needed to get the station wagon to the East. And there was no point in getting there before our furniture did anyhow. So we had lots of time to drive and to think.

The plane landing was smooth. We were supposed to

stay in our seats with the seat belts on until the plane stopped at the gate. The man in front of us didn't follow the rules. He was reaching up for his coat in the overhead compartment.

It did seem forever until we stopped. And then there was lots of confusion. People trying to get out in a hurry. People trying to get things from above, while others tried to push by in the aisle. Pete and I got our totes from the floor and onto the seats. Fortunately we didn't have overhead bags. We looked around for Dad.

"Wait for us," he was saying. I really couldn't hear him, but I knew he was saying it anyhow.

"OK," Dad directed, as he stemmed the tide in the aisle. "Carry your totes, and walk ahead of me." We obeyed. Mom and Justin followed us, with Dad bringing up the rear.

This time the pilot had invited us into the cockpit to see the new plane. But Dad said to keep going. Pete looked disappointed. We left the plane and went through the covered walkway into the airport.

Dad had just started to tell us that he didn't expect Grandpa and Grandma to meet us when we saw them! Justin broke into a run, but his tote bag slowed him down to a jog. Still, he was the first one to get one of Pop's big *bear hugs*. Soon everyone was hugging everyone else and laughing.

"I didn't expect you to come," Dad said. "I told you we'd rent a car." But everybody could tell he was glad his parents were there!

"Hey, Sonny!" Grandpa was doing his imitation of an old man with a cracking voice who can't hear very well. "You think I'm old, do you? Too late for the old man to stay up?" He had everybody in the waiting room laughing. Especially us. He's probably in better shape than Dad! Except he has white hair.

"You win!" Dad agreed. "Let's go to the baggage check place. We each have a suitcase."

Since we got off the plane faster than the luggage, we had to wait.

"You look just the same," I said.

"And why not?" Grandma said. "All this sunshine and fruit and time to play!"

"But you've changed," Pops said, taking a good look at us. "Jennifer, you're a beautiful young lady!" I'm sure he thinks so.

"And Pete. Catching up with your mom, aren't you?" Pete lowered his tote bag to the floor and stood even taller.

"And Justin," he said, with a grin like Dad's, "I sorta thought you'd be bigger."

Justin hesitated only a second—long enough for me to pray silently that he wouldn't feel hurt. "Well, Pops," he said, with a matching grin, "I sort of thought so too!" He laughed, and so did everyone else. Grandpa put his arm around Justin's shoulder, and they walked over to where the luggage was starting down the slide.

"They're all here but mine," Dad said. "Sue, you wait here," he told Mom, "and I'll check on the car rental."

But when he returned, his suitcase still hadn't come. One tan garment bag and some golf clubs were the only things left to be claimed.

"I can't believe it," Dad said. "We checked all five bags at the same time. And it was a nonstop flight." He went over to complain to someone who had *authority*.

"Your condo is close to ours," Grandma told Mom. "You know you could have stayed with us."

"We know," Mom said. "But Peter thought with the kids getting bigger we'd all have more space. The rental came up just when we needed it. And, of course, we still can be together during the day."

"Can we take turns sleeping at Grandma's?" Pete asked. "Like we did when we were little?"

"Just what I had in mind, Pete," Grandma said. "Would you like to be first and come with us tonight?"

"Great!" Pete said. Justin and I smiled. We knew we'd get turns later.

Dad came back. He was not grinning. "They sent my suitcase to Atlanta. They'll have it out to the condo in the morning." He turned to Grandpa. "Can you squeeze us all in for the ride over to the car rental?"

Grandpa looked at the four suitcases, the five totes, and the five extra Greens. "Hmmmmmmmm," he said. "The spirit is willing, but the car is small."

"You're right," Dad smiled. "Why don't you take one of the kids, and we'll meet you at the condo."

"I'll go, Dad," Pete said, picking up his suitcase and tote. "I'm sleeping with them tonight anyway. OK?"

When the rest of us drove off in the rented Chrysler, there were four totes and only three suitcases in the big trunk.

"I still can't believe it," Dad said.

"You can use my toothbrush," Justin offered.

"Yuck," said Dad.

I don't know how late it was when we finally got to Grandma and Grandpa's condo. Pretty late, I think.

"Need some pajamas?" Grandpa asked Dad. "You could pin the pants if they're too big."

"I probably couldn't squeeze my little toe inside," Dad said. They tease each other all the time.

"Maybe you'd like mine?" said Pete. "The only trouble is, I'm already wearing them."

"I'll manage," Dad laughed. "Come on, gang. We'll see you in the morning. What time is breakfast?"

"Let's make it brunch at nine-thirty," said Grandma. "I baked a couple of coffee cakes."

"You didn't," Mom said.

"From scratch," said Grandma. Not bragging. Just matter of fact.

When I curled up in bed, I was actually smiling. I am so happy. It is just exactly like it used to be. Except, of course, for Dad's suitcase. Fortunately, the condos each have two bathrooms.

8

Up and
at 'Em

Lord, it's me, Jennifer.

When I woke up this morning, I didn't know where I was. Sunshine was creeping in around the edge of the window shade. The green wallpaper didn't look familiar.

I listened, but I couldn't hear anything. Then Grandma giggled, and I sat up in bed fast. Grabbing my robe from the foot of the bed, I headed out to the living room. Justin and Grandma were sitting on a couch drinking orange juice and laughing their heads off.

"Hi, Jennifer," Grandma said.

"What are you doing here?" I asked. "I don't mean to be rude, but aren't you having company for breakfast?" I went over and gave her a kiss.

"I'm all ready, but my company hasn't come yet," she said.

I glanced at my watch. I couldn't believe it. Nine thirty-five.

"Grandma and I were just going to leave you a note that I was kidnapped," Justin said.

"By gypsies," Grandma added. "But he didn't think you'd buy that, so we were trying to think of something else." She giggled again. It is one of those laughs that is catching. Also it is rather loud. This time Mom stuck her head out.

"I can't believe it!" she said.

"Believe it," said Justin. "We really are here!"

"That's not exactly what I meant," Mom said. "We must have been exhausted. Your father is still sleeping."

"Don't wake him," Grandma said. "Jay and Pete have gone to get bait. When they get back, those who are ready can eat. Justin and I will head on down. OK?"

"I'll be down in five minutes," I said. "Don't go fishing without me." They didn't say anything. "Promise?" I said.

"Promise," said Grandma.

Back in my room, I dug through my suitcase for my underwear. Naturally, it was on the bottom, and I got everything messed up and out of order. Mom wouldn't *approve*. I grabbed a T-shirt and shorts and sneakers and closed the suitcase so she wouldn't see. Then I pulled the bedspread up and tried to smooth down the bumps. Nothing would pass inspection, I knew. But maybe, just maybe, she wouldn't *inspect*. I left the shade down.

"I'm going down, Mom," I said. She was talking to Dad, but I couldn't tell what they were saying.

As soon as I stood on the landing outside our condo, I could hear the boat motor. I hurried down the stairs and around the corner of the building. I was just in time to see Grandpa Green tossing a rope to Pete.

"Good morning, Pops," I said.

"You mean *good afternoon,* don't you?" Grandpa said. "We've been up for hours. Not like some people I could mention."

"Have you eaten?"

"Grandma wouldn't let us." Grandpa grinned. "A puny glass of juice so far. Where is everybody, anyway?"

"Justin's with Grandma. I'm here. And the folks are coming in a few minutes," I reported.

"Wash your hands good," Grandma said when we entered her condo.

"Yes, Mother," said Grandpa.

"Don't call me 'Mother,'" said Grandma. "I'm not your mother."

"Then don't sound like it," said Grandpa. "A man of my advanced years does not need to be told how to wash his hands." He grinned. "Come on, Pete. Let's wash our hands good."

Justin was already sitting at the table. "What have I missed?" he asked.

"Just some *man talk,*" said Pete. "You'll get your turn."

Well, Dad must have dressed with the speed of light, because he and Mom walked in just as we were sitting down at the table. He wore his same clothes.

"Good morning," Dad said. He had skipped shaving.

"Oh," Grandpa said, "is it morning already?" I think that's an *in joke*. The adults laughed knowingly, and we laughed because they were all laughing. Although didn't know why.

Grandpa and Grandma just assumed we were going to pray. They bowed their heads. We all did too.

"Lord, thanks for this beautiful day You've given us. Thanks for our family, and the joy we have in being together. Be close to those who aren't here, and remind them that You love them. And thanks for this food. We commit our day and ourselves to You. Amen."

When Pops prays, you just know he *means business*. And that he's talking to You. I don't think he's even aware that the rest of us are there.

Grandma told everyone who hadn't had orange juice to start in, and she went into the kitchen. She must have had everything ready, because she started putting all this great stuff on the pass-through.

There were platters of bacon, a plate of French toast, fresh strawberries, an omelette, and two of her famous homemade coffee cakes. Frankly it was the greatest breakfast I've ever had.

"Pete and I already got the shrimp," Grandpa said. Shrimp is what we use for bait. Not big ones like in restaurants, though. "Anyone else want to go fishing?"

49

"I do," I said. I could hardly wait.

"Me too," said Justin.

"I'm all set," said Grandma. She was dressed in apple green bermudas, a designer T-shirt, and white sneakers. Just in case anybody thinks she sticks to aprons! "In fact," she added, "I have the sandwiches all made."

"I think I'd better stay here to wait for my suitcase," Dad said. "Hope that's OK."

"Whatever," said Grandpa. "How about you, Sue?"

Mom said she thought she'd wait with Dad. "I think I'll enjoy a day by the pool. And I have a new book. I hope you won't mind having all the children?" she said.

"Are you kidding?" said Grandpa. "We've been waiting for this for months!"

"Well," said Dad, "Sue and I haven't been alone for months." He didn't look too unhappy about the prospect.

"Just a suggestion, Peter." Grandpa looked very serious. "If you want to borrow some clothes, feel free. And my razor is in the bathroom."

Dad burst out laughing. "Wouldn't you know," he said. "I thought I finally had an excuse to grow a beard."

"Not in this house." Grandpa was smiling. Pete and Justin looked at the men, grinning at each other.

"Hey," said Pete. "Did you ever fight about hair?"

Grandpa just laughed and shook his head. "Think we'd tell you? Is nothing in this world to be secret anymore?"

And that's all either one of them would say.

9

Out on the Boat

Lord, it's me, Jennifer.

Grandma has this thing about hats. She has a collection of them in the garage, and everyone who goes out on the boat gets to pick one. There are all styles and shapes and colors. No one ever refuses a hat. Grandma wouldn't let them!

"I'm going to be a cowboy today," Justin said. The hat rested on his ears, but nobody laughed. At least not in the beginning. Suddenly Grandma was laughing so hard we thought she'd fall over.

"Would you consider being a baseball player?" she gasped.

"Never," said Justin.

I picked a Chicago Cubs cap and put it on backwards. Pete chose an old straw hat. Pops wore his *fishing hat* — the one he always wears. And Grandma chose a sombrero "to match her shorts." She looked like a lamp.

Well, everyone was already laughing before we even got into the boat. With that kind of mood, sunny weather, and picnic lunch, we knew the day would be great.

As Grandpa eased the boat through the canals, we waved at Mom and Dad. They were standing on the balcony waving at us. I hoped Dad's luggage would come.

"Want to steer, Pete?" Grandpa gave my brother the wheel, stood behind him, and made suggestions in a soft voice. "Great job!" he said. "Let me have it now."

Once we were out of the canal, we could use the big motor. I watched the buildings get smaller. Even the condos looked like toy blocks.

"Are we going to the island?" Justin asked.

"I think we'll try that first," Pops said. When he got kind of near, he let the motor die and reached for the fishing poles. He's got more poles than Grandma has hats! He let each of us choose one. They were all ready to go—except for bait.

"I'll get the bait bucket," Pete offered. He put it in the middle where everyone could reach it. I was glad it was shrimp. Frankly, I'm not sure I could handle worms!

Pete got his line in first at the back of the boat. I wasn't watching when he did it. Grandma's went into the water on the left side.

I stuck on the shrimp and tried to remember how to cast my line in. I cocked my arm and tossed. Nothing happened. How embarrassing. The shrimp just hung there over the water.

"You forgot to release it, Jennifer," Pops reminded. He came over and patiently explained how to do it. Success! My line was next to Grandma's.

Almost the minute Justin's line got in the water there was a jerk. "I've got one!" he yelled.

"Good boy," said Grandpa, moving over to his side.

Justin reeled in. "Oh, no," he said.

"Cleaned your hook," said Pops. "Here, let's see if we can get him with this one." He showed Justin how to bait the hook more securely.

Pete didn't say anything. He just sat quietly, almost as if he didn't know the rest of us were out there too. I didn't see the tug at his line. But we all saw the pole bending and Pete reeling.

"Easy," said Grandpa. "Don't let him get away. Take your time. You have him. It's a beauty!" He joined Pete at the rear of the boat. He held the net in his right hand. "Got him," he yelled.

Grandma stuck her rod in a holder and grabbed for her camera. Every fish, little or big, gets his picture taken. It is part of the *routine*. "Hold him closer to the camera," she advised. "That way he'll look bigger!" Pete stood there smiling.

"Wonderful," said Pops.

Justin reeled in his line. He was headed for the back of

the boat when his hat fell off. He left it. And, as soon as Pete cast again, Justin was right behind him. In fact, on top of him. The line, that is.

It was a *tense moment*. Suddenly Grandma's high little voice started to sing. "I will make you fishers of men, fishers of men, fishers of men ..."

Grandpa stopped and joined in. "I will make you fishers of men ..."

All of us Green kids helped finish "... if you'll follow me."

Grandpa looked at us. "You know it?" he said.

"Well, sure," I said. "Doesn't everybody?"

"Here, Son," Pops said to Justin. "Let me have that for a minute. I think I can get them untangled."

Justin looked kind of embarrassed. "I'm sorry," he said.

"It's OK," Pete said. "There's room for both of us."

Pops worked carefully. Finally he handed Justin's pole back to him. "Try it now," he said.

"I've got one. I've got one," Grandma squealed.

"For goodness sakes, Mary, you'll scare it to death!" He captured her fish in the net and worked the hook out of its mouth.

"Let me take your picture," said Justin. He put his pole in the holder near Pete. "What do I do?"

"Wipe your hands first," said Grandma, giving him a towel. She showed him where to look and what to push. "Can you see me?" She held her small fish at arm's length so it would look bigger.

"Hey, that's fun," Justin said. He picked up his hat.

By lunchtime, everyone except me had caught a fish—even Justin. His picture was hilarious. The hat made him look all the smaller—even his fish looked big.

Grandma wiped her hands and got out the lunch basket. There were peanut butter and jelly sandwiches, meat, and tuna salad. Grandma remembered how I love tuna salad.

Well, it turns out that they even pray on boats! "Would one of you like to *return thanks?*" said Pops.

I volunteered. I guessed that *returning thanks* just meant praying. "Lord," I said, "thanks for this special time with Pops and Grandma. Thanks for this food. And please help me catch a fish this afternoon. Amen."

"Does He do that?" Pete asked.

"Do what?" Grandma wondered.

"Help people catch fish?"

"Well, sure," Grandma replied. She sounded so much like me that everybody laughed.

Well, it didn't happen right away. Pete even caught a fish while he was eating his sandwich, if You can believe that! He had to unhook his pole, reel it in, net it, take out the hook, and put it on the stringer. And then, of course, wash his hands good. We skipped the photo.

I won't explain Grandma's method for going to the bathroom on the boat, because it is too private. (It does involve her holding up a sheet.)

When the fish stopped biting near the island, Grandpa tried other spots. He knows dozens of them. It is rumored in the family that he has never come back from fishing empty handed.

Although I baited my hook right and did everything Pops told me, I never did catch one fish. I was disappointed, and I was embarrassed.

"Jennifer," Pops said, "I think everyone's tired, and your folks will be expecting us for dinner. Will you understand if we go back? Maybe you'll have better luck next time."

"He didn't do it," I said.

"Who didn't do what?" Grandpa asked.

"Help me catch a fish. He didn't answer my prayer."

"Sometimes, Jennifer," Grandpa said, "God says no."

Well, I guess I already knew that. But frankly it was kind of embarrassing. Here I was giving You a chance to show them we're such good friends, and You didn't come through! Was there a reason?

"It's Mom and Dad!" Pete yelled. "And Dad has on different pants and shirt. His suitcase must have come." We had just rounded the turn into the canal which leads to the condo. Everybody waved from the boat. Pete held up the stringer of fish.

When we docked, Grandma handed the camera to Mom. "Here," she said, "would you please take a picture of all of us?" We adjusted our hats, held up all the fish, and grinned.

I think I'll remember that day always anyhow, Lord. But, just in case, there we all were. Including Grandma, who looked just like a *lamp*.

56

10

Take Two
and Smile

Lord, it's me, Jennifer.

In case You mention this to any girls, Lord, don't tell
them I don't help clean the fish! Grandpa and Dad seem
to think it is men's work, and my brothers go along with
it. And, frankly, it's so yucky that I'm just as glad to get
out of it. That's the honest truth. Some things aren't
worth *taking a stand* on.

Which is why I went up to the condo with Mom and
Grandma.

"Where shall we eat?" Grandma asked. On days when
she goes fishing, she doesn't cook.

"Is Ben's Beanery still in business?" Mom wondered.

Grandma smiled. "Still growing," she said. Ben started

out with this little hole-in-the wall diner, and now it's a huge restaurant.

"Grandma," I said, as I left to take my shower, "remember when we used to have lunch together?"

"Of course I do, Jennifer," she said. "Would you like to do that some day this week?"

"Could we? Just the two of us?" I glanced nervously at Mom. "I don't want you to feel left out," I said.

"Don't be silly," said Mom. "I have you all year."

Suddenly I realized that most of our time together is spent doing things that aren't really fun—like her driving me places. I wonder if I asked her to have lunch with me if she'd do it?

We all gathered on the sidewalk next to our rental car at six-fifteen. Pops and Dad wore sport shirts without ties. So did Pete and Justin. Mom, Grandma, and I wore cotton skirts.

"I can't believe it's the end of October," Dad said. "The weather here is beautiful. It must be the world's best-kept secret."

When we got to Ben's, I was expecting to wait in line, but we were seated right away. "Not quite like spring vacation, is it?" Pops said.

"Hardly," Dad agreed.

"This is my treat," Grandpa said, as we opened our menus. "You kids can have anything you want."

"Anything?" I asked. "Even lobster?"

"Jennifer!" Mom said.

"I said anything," Grandpa repeated. "How's she going to know if she likes it if she never tastes it?"

"You're impossible to argue with," said Dad.

"I always was," said Pops.

Well, I got my lobster, with the little dish of melted butter to dip it in. Now I know I like it. Dad and Grandpa both got prime rib, and I noticed it cost as much as the lobster. But I didn't say anything. Pete picked steak. Mom and Grandma ordered Veal Oscar. And Justin wanted a hamburger.

"Get something better," I whispered.

"Why?" said Justin. "I like hamburgers."

"Suit yourself," I said. He's probably too young for Ben's Beanery. The waitress left.

"Hey, what do you call a cow with no legs?" Pops said. Nobody could guess.

"Ground beef!" said Grandpa. Justin didn't catch on at first, but then he laughed harder than anyone else.

"Did you hear that Willie Nelson got hit by a car?" Dad said.

"No," said Grandpa.

"Well, he was on the road again!" said Dad.

"Oh, no," said Mom.

The waitress came with our salads. There was this awkward pause. I just knew Pops was going to pray. I mean, they are really religious.

"Let's pray," Grandpa said. He didn't seem embarrassed at all. Just bowed his head. So everybody else did too. It was a little hard to hear him. "Thanks, Lord, for a beautiful day together. Thank You for this food, and bless our evening together."

I didn't hear him say "Amen," so I kept my head bowed and my eyes closed. I kept waiting. When I peeked, I realized he was done. I attacked my salad without looking at anyone.

We even got dessert. Except for Mom and Grandma. They said no because of diets.

The waitress brought Dad the check. "Give it to the old man over there," he said, grinning. Pops chuckled and took out his wallet.

"Who's for some Uno?" Grandma invited. We almost always play a game after dinner. It is a *tradition*.

We gathered around the table, with Dad and Pops on the ends of the oval, since they have the longest arms. Dad shuffled, dealt out seven cards each, and the *competition* was on.

The *point* is to *go out first*. That's easier said than done. We are very competitive. Even Grandma. She likes to catch people who don't say "Uno" when they get down to their last card. "Take two!" she says. "You didn't say it!"

"Oh, no!" said Pete. He got stuck with two wild cards at the end. He was losing anyway.

"Don't give up, Son," Pops said. "There's always another hand." He was right. The next time Pete went out and stuck Pops with a "Draw Four" at the end. They were fighting each other for *last place* and laughing as if they were ahead. Usually Pete isn't that good a sport.

The game can change before you know it. I zoomed from *first place to fourth*. I pretended I didn't care.

Mom is kind of quiet. Doesn't say much. Then, all of a sudden, she plays a "Reverse," and you'd think it's the ninth inning at Veterans' Stadium. I mean we are noisy! But, since Grandma and Pops don't seem to mind, Mom and Dad don't either. If playing cards with your grandparents sounds boring, you haven't been in on a game with *three generations* of Greens!

"Well," said Dad, who hates to lose, "I'll get you tomorrow night!"

"We'll see," said Grandma.

"It's my turn to sleep here," said Justin. I nodded. "I'll be right back with my stuff," he said. Dad went with him.

"What time is church?" Mom asked. She and Dad always go in Florida.

"Early service is eight-thirty," said Grandma. "But I think the nine-forty-five will be fine. Church isn't as crowded out of season."

"What time do you want us down for breakfast?" Mom wondered.

"Let's say eight o'clock," Grandma replied. "Unless that's too early?"

"That's just fine," Mom said.

It didn't sound as if we were going to Sunday school, Lord. But I'm glad my brothers have *experience* going to church. I hope my parents *like it*. I can just picture all of us sitting in a row together. Even the thought makes me feel warm inside and glad.

61

11

Family Service

Lord, it's me, Jennifer.

Church in Florida is sort of like going to a restaurant. The men don't dress up. Unless you call wearing a clean sport shirt *dressing up*. Personally, I don't. In Philadelphia, the men wear suits and ties.

Another thing different is that there are lots of old people. Especially in the fall. During spring vacation there are some kids. But this time there were hardly any.

All the kids in church know our grandparents! Wouldn't you think that out of all those old people there would be plenty to go around? But no. They all swarmed around Grandma and Pops as if they belonged to them. I hate to admit this, but I felt jealous.

"Look, Grandpa Green!" A little blond ran up to show him her Sunday-school papers. He looked, smiled, and she was satisfied.

"Can you come, Grandma Green?" This time it was a girl about Pete's size, with some sort of invitation.

"I'll call you, dear," said Grandma.

"Did you see me?" asked a boy with two front teeth missing.

"I sure did, Adam," Grandpa said. "You were positively sensational!"

Well, we could hardly get out to shake hands with the minister. "Morning, Bill," Pops said to a man younger than Dad. "I'd like you to meet our family. Our son, Peter. Our daughter-in-law, Sue. And our grandchildren, Jennifer, Pete, and Justin."

Dad stuck out his hand and said, "Fine sermon!" The rest of us just smiled.

"Fine young man," Pops said. "A real student of the Word." Sometimes Grandpa calls the Bible that. I'm not sure why.

"How about a fish fry for lunch?" Grandma asked when we got in the car.

"Did we catch enough?" Pete wondered.

"Well, almost enough. I'll sneak in a few frozen from last week."

No other fish, even lobster, tastes as good as eating the ones you've caught. Even though, strictly speaking, I didn't happen to catch any of these. I think just being on the boat counts!

"Tell us about when you were a little boy," Pete said after lunch. We had to wait an hour before we could go swimming.

Grandpa laughed. "Where shall I begin?"

"At the beginning," I said.

"Well," Pops said, "I was the youngest of seven children. They had just about run out of names by then. But my mother wanted to call me J. Templeton Green. She figured if she named me that I'd be successful!"

"What does the J. stand for, Grandpa?" Justin asked.

"Don't you know?"

"I thought your name was Jay," he said.

"Nope, although that's what people call me. It stands for Justin."

"How did you get into the furniture business?" Pete asked.

"I went to work for the owner of the store. Unpacked crates." He smiled at Grandma. "And then I married the owner's daughter. The owner's beautiful daughter! But I still unpacked crates," he laughed. "At least at first."

"Were you disappointed that I didn't want to work in the store?" Dad asked.

"Well, sort of. But your mom and I know that everybody is different. Each person should have a turn trying what he's best at. And you were always taking things apart."

"Do you take things apart?" Justin asked Dad.

"Not now," Dad laughed. "But we must have had a million radios spread all over the basement."

"Only because you didn't have time to fix them," Grandma defended. "You were too busy in sports."

"Were you a jock too, Pops?" Pete asked.

"Heavens no!" Grandpa said. "I couldn't walk around without falling down. That's why we got such a kick out of your dad. He sure didn't take after me!"

"Like I don't take after Dad," Pete said.

"Exactly," Grandpa agreed. "Nothing to be ashamed of. The glory doesn't last long anyhow. Right, Peter?"

"Right," Dad agreed. "Not many men my age play football or basketball anymore."

"Now, take fishing," Pops said. "There's a sport you can enjoy all your life." No one disagreed.

"I was just thinking," Pete said. "Isn't it funny? I'm named after Dad, who was good in sports. And Justin is named after Grandpa, who wasn't good in sports."

"Were we mixed up when we were little?" Justin asked. Everyone laughed.

"How about Jennifer who is good in writing?" Pete asked.

"She probably was adopted," Justin said. Even I laughed.

"Tell us about Aunt Elizabeth," I said.

Suddenly everybody was very quiet.

"I think it's time to go swimming," Dad said. "Get your suits on and go on down. We'll watch from the balcony."

I really was *too old* to fall for that dodge. But I went anyway.

12

My Turn

Lord, it's me, Jennifer.

It was "my turn" to sleep over with Grandma and Pops. I had looked forward to it from the beginning, but now I felt nervous. Like being called on in class. Or waiting to play in a recital.

There was so much I wanted them to know. But I didn't know how to start telling them.

"Remember when we used to have a cocoa party?" Grandma said.

I remembered. "We all put on our robes. And we turned off most of the lights." Funny how I had forgotten. Now I remembered everything, but especially the feeling of closeness and belonging.

"Last one ready is a rotten egg," said Pops.

"No fair, Jay. I have to make the cocoa," said Grandma.

"You're right," my grandfather agreed. "First one ready turns out the lights."

Once we sat down around the big coffee table with our cocoa and the dim light, talking wasn't really a problem. In fact, once we got started, I thought we might just talk all night. There was so much to say.

"How do you like Philadelphia?" Grandpa asked.

I thought a minute. "It's funny," I said. "When Dad first told us we'd be moving there, I couldn't even imagine what it would be like. I felt all mixed up. Part of me was excited to try a new adventure, but part of me wanted to stay where I had always been."

Pops nodded. "But you decided to go."

"I had *no choice,*" I said.

"And how is it now that you're there?" Grandma asked.

"To be honest, I really like it." That is the truth. "The summer was long, because we didn't have many friends. But now it is getting harder and harder to remember my old life in Illinois. It seems like a dream."

"We know what you mean, Jennifer. We've been retired here for almost four years," Grandma said.

"But you didn't have to leave," I said. "You had a choice. Wasn't it hard?"

"Yes and no," Grandpa explained. "In our case, the Lord nudged us. We prayed about it a lot. Uncle Bob didn't need me at the store. He needed the freedom to make his own decisions. Some guys don't know enough to quit."

"And, after my hip operation, I couldn't be on my feet too long," Grandma added. "Our house was too big, and the yard was too much for us."

Grandpa grinned. "And, there was always the fishing."

I had to say it. "But you left us," I said. "How could you leave your grandchildren?" It was something I never did understand. They loved us so much.

"You're right, Jennifer," Grandma said. "That was the hardest part. But we figured you'd come for visits. Sometimes when you have to make more of an effort, getting together becomes more special."

"And, of course, we didn't really abandon you," Grandpa said. "We pray for you every day—sometimes many times! The Lord is with you."

"Sure," I said, "but you didn't know that then."

"We knew that He loved you—even more than we do. As a matter of fact, we nagged at your parents to take you to Sunday school every time we saw them. It was spoiling our relationship," Grandma said. "So we came down here and prayed twice as hard."

"You mean," I said, "that God answered your prayer when Mom and Dad made us go to Sunday school?"

"That's one way of looking at it," Pops said. "We didn't tell the Lord how to do it—just to make himself and His love real to you."

"No kidding?" I said. All of a sudden I felt goose

bumps on my legs and arms. Even with my robe on.

"Uncle Bob's family was so excited. They could hardly wait to tell us last spring," Grandma said.

"How did you feel when we went to Philadelphia?"

"Well," Grandma admitted, "at first we were tempted to ask if the Lord knew what He was doing. But we know He is faithful. So we just kept on trusting Him."

"I'm a Christian," I said. I just blurted it out like that.

Grandma started to cry because she was so happy. And we all hugged each other.

"This calls for more cocoa," Pops announced.

"I'll get it," Grandma said. "But wait for me."

They wanted to know everything. So I told them about the Harringtons inviting us to Sunday school and church. And about my Sunday-school class in Pennsylvania. And about youth group. And, of course, about the *retreat*. "I haven't told Dad and Mom," I admitted. "I've been waiting for the *right time,* but it hasn't happened yet."

"It will." Grandpa sounded confident. "God is always faithful. Just wait for Him. And keep praying."

"I have so many other things to tell you," I said. "I'm taking riding lessons." I told them all about my day with the borrowed horse. They both laughed so hard.

Finally, Grandma said she was fading. "Another big day on the boat tomorrow," she reminded us.

I went to bed. But I couldn't go to sleep. "Amazing!" I thought. And then my mind said, "Amazing Grace." Lord, who is Grace anyhow?

That's the last thing I remember thinking.

13

The Big Fish

Lord, it's me, Jennifer.

Today everybody went out on the boat to fish. Naturally, everyone had to wear hats. But, except for Pops, who always wears the same cap, everybody picked different ones. Dad surprised us by giving Grandma a Phillies cap to add to her collection. Pete wore it.

The rest of us had fun choosing. It is sort of like Halloween without the candy. Dad wore a golf cap with two crossed golf clubs on the front. Mom wore a calico bonnet with her Calvin Klein jeans. Justin gave up on his cowboy routine and settled for an Irish cap (which also came down over his ears). Grandma wore a red beret. And I wore a pink straw hat.

There is plenty of room for everyone on the boat. It is not fancy, at least that's what Pops says, but it is nearly thirty feet long. We chugged through the canal on the peewee motor. It is *a rule* that boats can't use big motors in the canals.

"Why does your father wear two pairs of pants when he plays golf?" asked Grandpa.

"Do you?" Justin asked.

"Of course not. It's a joke," Dad explained. "OK, why?"

"In case he gets a hole in one," Grandpa laughed.

"You know, Dad, that's really terrible," my father said.

"And I don't even get it," said Justin. Everyone laughed even harder. I didn't get it either, but I *faked it*.

Grandpa tried a different spot today. It was farther away. I just sat back and listened to the noise of the motor and enjoyed the feel of the sunshine on my face. I hope I'm getting tan.

It was a perfect day to fish. To tell the truth, any day is a perfect day to fish if you are catching a lot. And we were. Grandpa had hardly handed out the poles when I got a strike! I was afraid I'd lose him, but I didn't. Grandpa smiled as he helped with the net. "Sometimes you just have to be patient," he said. I nodded.

I will say this. I think Grandpa has more fun when other people catch fish than when he does! With everyone pulling them in so fast, Pops spent most of the morning running around with the net, getting out hooks, and putting fish on the stringer. Once there was so much excitement we nearly forgot to take a picture!

I couldn't believe it when Grandma said it was time for lunch. It seemed like we had just started. That shows you how many fish we caught!

"Can I help?" Mom offered. Grandma said no—everybody could help themselves. When we all had our sandwiches, Grandpa asked if anyone would like to pray.

"I will," said Dad. I nearly dropped my sandwich! Justin and Pete were glancing at me, so I was a *good example* and closed my eyes. Besides, I didn't really want to look at Dad or Mom.

"Lord," Dad said, "thanks for this beautiful day, and this chance to be together. And bless the food. Amen."

I tried to act casual—as if it happened all the time. For as You know, Lord, my father never prays anything except the memorized one we always say at mealtime. I didn't know he could!

Well, everyone got over the shock and started eating and talking about what a good fishing spot we had. Dad took off his golf cap, smoothed back his hair, and put the hat on again.

By the time we finished our pop and chips and cookies, we saw that three other boats had joined us. And a small rowboat was heading our way.

"I've got one!" Pete yelled. Grandpa sat down beside him as he reeled it in. "It feels like a huge one!"

"Shhh," said Grandma, looking at the other boats. But Pete didn't hear her. He was too busy concentrating.

"Let him have a little line," Pops said. "Easy . . . Oh, my goodness!"

"Don't let him get away," yelled Dad. Naturally Pete wouldn't if he could help it.

All the rest of us stopped to watch. While the fish was flopping around in the bottom of the boat, Grandpa was moving fast with the net.

My brother was grinning from ear to ear. I've seen bigger fish mounted on walls in restaurants, but this looked like a *record size* for our family. It was so big that Pete didn't even have to hold it closer to the camera. After Justin took the picture, Grandma took an extra one, *just in case*.

It was wonderful. We thought so, and so did the other people in the boats around us.

"OK, pull in your lines," Grandpa ordered. We obeyed. Before we knew what was happening, Pops had started the big motor full blast and was steering between two rowboats. Leaving a churning wake behind us, we headed for another spot.

"Dad, I'm surprised at you," my father said.

"Normally I wouldn't do that," Pops said. "But they were getting so close they were *rude!*"

Well, whether that changed our luck or not, I can't say. But we weren't catching fish anymore.

"We've got a lot of cleaning to do," said Grandpa. "Let's head back." And everybody agreed.

I looked around at each person in our family. Pete was smiling all the time.

14

Grandma's
Mr. Wonderful

Lord, it's me, Jennifer.

Cleaning the fish took a long time, all right. We knew it would.

"Sue, have a rest, dear," Grandma said. "You look tired."

"I don't know how you keep going like this," Mom said.

"I have all year to rest up," Grandma laughed. "Jennifer and I will bake cookies. Want to, Jennifer?"

I did. Doing anything with Grandma is fun. We decided on oatmeal chocolate chip, a family favorite. But Grandma also had another idea. She had me rolling other dough into little balls. I knew we were making Santa cookies. Normally, we make them only for Christmas.

"It's a *special treat,*" Grandma explained. "Don't tell."

I didn't. We were all finished and had the dishwasher going when the guys came in. Grandma offered each a chocolate chip cookie and a glass of milk. "To tide you over till dinner," she explained.

We ate at the Seafood Shanty. I ordered steak. Everybody thought it was dumb for me to pick steak at a fish restaurant.

"Now, never you mind, Jennifer," Pops said, when I started getting upset. "Just let them tease. Just smile, and pick what you want." So I did.

Justin, who probably was copying me, ordered lobster, much to Dad's surprise. But Grandpa told my brother the same thing he told me. Justin ended up dribbling butter down his face and shirt.

The adults all ordered whitefish. It's a Seafood Shanty specialty. Pete, still basking in the glow of catching a whopper, ordered shrimp with a double order of cocktail sauce.

"Remember the first year you were down here?" Mom said. "We drove down during spring break. You packed our fish in a Styrofoam cooler to take home."

"And it leaked!" Pete remembered. "Whew, what a smell!"

"And Dad bought new underpants on sale," I remembered.

"They were in the trunk in a red bag next to the

cooler," Mom said. "And, by the time we found them, the bag had faded all over them!" Even Justin, who probably didn't remember, was laughing.

"I bleached and bleached, but you had tie-dyed under-pants for months!"

We were all laughing so hard, especially my father, that even the waitress started laughing. "Want to sit down and join us?" Dad asked.

We skipped dessert because we had the cookies to eat while we played cards. I kept forgetting to say "Uno," so I lost.

"My turn to sleep over," said Pete.

"I think not," Dad said. Pete looked disappointed. "We'll have your grandparents so exhausted they won't want us to come back."

I looked at Pops. Then at Grandma. They did look pretty tired.

That's why we all went back to our own condo. But even with the five of us there, we didn't seem like much of a group. Suddenly the evening seemed *boring*.

The next morning we had a pancake-eating contest! It was Grandma's idea, and she did the cooking. We are all, except Mom, so competitive that no one wanted to lose. I wasn't about to admit I was full, and neither was anyone else. Finally, Grandma had to declare the contest *a tie*. And we all had terrible stomachaches.

Well, it wasn't a good day to go out in the boat. It looked like rain. Grandma said it was a perfect day to read and do puzzles. She got out a jigsaw puzzle with something like 3,000 pieces. Count me out! I remembered to smile, as I excused myself to go get a book.

In the afternoon it cleared up. Everyone, including Grandma, put on bathing suits and swam in the gulf.

Grandma announced at supper that Friday night was going to be a special secret! She glanced at me to make sure I wouldn't tell. Frankly, I don't think Santa cookies are that big a deal, but I wouldn't tell her that!

Everything we did all week was fun. If we caught fish, it was fun. If we didn't, then something else was fun. I wondered what it must have been like, growing up in Dad's family. He was the oldest. Next came Uncle Bob. And then came Aunt Elizabeth.

I wondered again about Aunt Elizabeth. She was in my parent's wedding pictures, standing on the front-porch stairs with everyone else. She was just a girl then. My age? It was hard to tell.

◆ ◆ ◆ ◆

On the day Grandma and I went out together for lunch, Dad took Mom out. To a different restaurant, of course. Pops took Pete and Justin to "Hamburger Heaven."

I copied Grandma and ordered something called quiche—a good word to remember next time we play Scrabble. It is pronounced "keesh." She said men aren't supposed to like it! Personally, I don't know why they wouldn't. It is delicious.

Grandma let me have a cup of tea at the end of the meal. She said women do that so they can talk.

"Did you always like Grandpa—from the very beginning when you met him?" I asked.

"I did," she said. "He was my 'Mr. Wonderful' all through high school. Not necessarily the best looking. But he had *staying power*."

"What's that?" I asked.

"Oh, it's hard to explain," Grandma said. "I'd like someone else for a while, but I'd always keep coming back to Jay. The longer I knew him, the more I liked him."

"When did you get married?" I wondered.

"Well, he went away to college for a time. And I studied Home Economics. Then Mama wanted me to stay home with her for a year. So, of course, I did."

"It sounds like you knew each other a long time."

"Oh my, yes," she agreed. "But we both had lots of growing up to do. You know, maturing."

"You mean you waited until you were sure he really was Mr. Wonderful?" I asked.

"We waited until I didn't expect him always to be Mr. Wonderful. I knew he loved me, and I loved him, and we both loved the Lord. The promises we made were 'until death us do part,' promises we have always kept."

"Isn't it hard to keep a promise like that?" I wondered. "Forever is a long time."

"I love him more today than I did the day we were married," she said. "We've been through a lot together, but we've always known we could count on each other. It seems to me it would be harder to live not knowing that."

I never thought of it that way. "How long has it been, Grandma?"

"Thirty-nine years!"

"Wow," I said. "When you get to forty, we'll have to have a party. By the way," I said, "would you like to hear about the Harrington boys?"

"Certainly," she said. And we both laughed.

15

Surprise
Party

Lord, it's me, Jennifer.

Something was going on. I suspected it had something to do with the plans for Friday night. It definitely had to do with more than cookies.

Grandma continued to play *recreation director,* and we kept having lots of fun. But Grandpa went on several unexplained errands. Grandma excused herself from a walk in the surf to take a nap. And there were other *signs* —quick knowing looks, grins, a buildup of excitement.

Dad and Mom seemed *in the dark* too.

"Hey, what's going on?" Dad asked.

"You'll see. Just be patient," Pops said.

The plans called for us to be ready to leave at six-thirty.

"Coats and ties?" Dad wondered.

"Never," said Grandpa.

We all stood there waiting when our grandparents came down. "We have reservations for six-fifty," said Grandma.

"Where?" Mom asked. "A new place?"

"Not really," Pops said. "Same management, but a new decor."

"What's decor?" Pete asked.

"How it looks," I told him.

"Which way?" Dad asked, when we all squeezed into the Chrysler.

"Turn left at the stoplight," Grandpa directed. "Now keep going." After fifteen minutes I was hopelessly lost. And I'm usually pretty good on directions.

"OK," said Grandma, "right at the next light."

"Hey," said Justin. "There's a condo just like ours."

"It is ours," Dad said. He pulled back into our parking space. "What is going on, anyway?"

"You'll see," said Grandma. "Everybody just wait here a minute, and when I wave, you can come up."

I could smell the turkey as we climbed the stairs. And a record was playing, "O Come, All Ye Faithful." It was Christmas in October!

Everybody got into the *spirit* and was wishing each other Merry Christmas and Happy New Year. Over in one corner, where the avocado plant usually sat, was an artificial Christmas tree, all decorated with ornaments. And, underneath were presents!

Grandma was wearing a red and green apron. "Surprised?"

"You can say that again," Dad said. That means he really was. "Now you kids can see where I got my flair for drama and surprises. I inherited it."

"Just don't blame everything on us," Grandpa laughed. "But we did have a lot of fun when the kids were growing up."

"Remember when you gave me the box of underwear?" Dad laughed.

"And you had asked for a basketball hoop," Grandpa said.

"Is underwear all he got?" Justin asked.

"Of course not," Pops laughed. "But you should have seen the look on his face!"

I remembered last Christmas, when I thought I was getting a horse. Instead, I got to pick out a new bedroom set. But I never told anyone in the family about that.

"Over the sand and through the surf, to Grandmother's condo we go," Dad sang. "They'll have to rewrite all those old songs," he said.

"Before I carve, I want everyone to see the bird," Grandpa said. He carried it around the room on a big platter. Just like Dad does at our house.

"I'd like to pray," I said, when we all sat down around the table. At first I felt embarrassed. But once I got going, I forgot the family was even there!

"Lord," I said, as You know, "this has been the neatest week! We all want to thank You for every single minute of it. Thank You for giving us such wonderful grandparents and such a neat family. And thank You for this wonderful dinner Grandma fixed. Joy to the world," I said. "Amen."

Well, we had our choice of light or dark meat, dressing, cranberries—the whole works. Even a choice of pie or Santa cookies for dessert. As usual, some of us ate too much. I won't mention names.

"If you had told us, we could have brought you your presents," Mom said after dinner.

"If we had told you, you wouldn't have been surprised," said Pops. He announced that he was going to be Santa. "I've missed seeing you open your gifts," he said. He had exactly the same grin that Dad wears when he passes out our presents. It was *weird*.

This time I was first. My gift was a large box. Grandma confessed that she had had a hard time wrapping it.

"Oh, great!" I said. "No more brown paper bags!" I got a beautiful sports tote bag. I was just starting to go over to kiss my grandparents, when Pops said I should open it up. Inside was a check, and a note telling me to use the money for riding clothes!

"I can't believe it!" I yelled. Not too ladylike, but *who cares?* "Now all I need is a horse!" I said. Everybody laughed.

Dad got a leather briefcase. He acted like he never had one before. "Wow, this is great!" he said. And he kissed Grandma and Pops also.

Justin's box was smaller. It took him only a minute to tear off the wrappings. "Wow!" he said. "My own camera. And film!" And he kissed our grandparents.

"You'll have to see if you can take pictures of anything besides fish," Grandpa said.

Pete's gift was long and skinny. I had a good idea what it was. Sure enough, he got a fishing pole and reel. "You've got to carry on the tradition," Pops said. Pete kissed him and Grandma and promised he would.

There were a small box and an envelope still under the tree. Naturally, we knew Mom was the only one who hadn't gotten anything. So it wasn't surprising that it was her turn. Grandpa gave her the envelope first. Personally, I thought it was going to be *a check*.

Wrong! Mom looked surprised and somewhat puzzled when she opened a printed folder.

"What is it?" Dad asked.

Grandma explained. "When you get home, you'll be receiving a special squirrel-proof bird feeder. That shows pictures of it. We heard there are lots of birds in your area."

"Lots of squirrels too," Mom laughed.

"They won't have a chance," Grandma said. "If they climb up to the porch of the feeder, the food supply is closed off. Pops and I hope you all enjoy the winter more by making friends with the chickadees."

"Thank you very much," Mom said.

"That's not all," said Pops, as Mom started to get up.

He handed her the tiny box.

"Oh, my goodness," said Mom, as she gently removed a ring. "How beautiful!" We all gathered around to look. It had a blue stone in the middle with little diamonds around the edge.

"It was my mother's," Grandpa said. "I want you to have it. We love you like a daughter, Sue. And you've given us a priceless gift—three beautiful grandchildren!"

Mom started to cry. And we all got tears in our eyes. Grandma passed Kleenex to everyone—even Dad.

"Can you come up in December for another Christmas with us in Pennsylvania?" Mom asked.

"I don't know," Grandma said. "Bob and Carol have been wanting us to come to Illinois. But holiday travel is such a hassle."

"Maybe we could go to Illinois too," Dad said. "It could be a family reunion. I'd be happy to have my secretary get all the tickets."

"Well," Pops said, "we'll think about it."

"Everybody stand by the tree," Justin said. "I want to take your picture." Grandma took some too. Our October Christmas was well recorded on film.

Before we left, Grandpa said it wouldn't be Christmas without the Christmas story. He reached for his nearly-worn-out Bible. I braced myself for the Wise-men and shepherds.

"'For God so loved the world that he gave his one and only Son, that whoever believes in him shall not perish but have eternal life.' That," Pops said, "is the greatest gift of all." I agree.

16

Home Again

Lord, it's me, Jennifer.

Saturday was our last day in Florida, and in the morning we all went on the boat. Pete caught a smallish fish with his new rod. He held it close to the camera when Justin took his picture. Both of my brothers were grinning. And so were Dad and Grandpa.

"We have to get these fish cleaned and frozen so you can take them along with the rest," Grandma said. "We'll have to head back early."

Mom did our laundry in Grandma's washer and dryer. That way we were able to pack clean clothes to take home. The suitcases stood in a row by the door before we went to bed. As I've said, Mom is *very organized.*

"Someone will come in and clean after we're gone," Dad explained. "It's part of the rental." Mom looked happy.

That night I dreamed the fish were thawing under my seat, and everyone on the plane was wondering what smelled!

"I just don't trust those airplane meals," Grandma said the next morning. "What if they only give you a drink and a little package of peanuts?" That's why we had breakfast together before we went to the airport.

I got to ride to the airport with Pops and Grandma. There was so much I wanted to say, but I really couldn't think of anything. "This has been the best week of my life," I said. "I love you both so much!"

"Remember that the Lord loves you too, dear. And we'll keep praying for you every day," Grandpa said. "Do you know Romans 8:28?"

"It sounds like a verse," I said. "But I'm not very into knowing their numbers yet."

"Of course not," Pops said. "But this is a good one to memorize. It tells us that 'in all things God works for the good of those who love Him.'"

"What was that number again?" I asked. I wrote it down on a paper in my purse.

Well, it was *hugging* and *kissing* time all over. Each of us kissed Grandma and Pops at least twice.

"Don't forget to consider Christmas," Mom said.

Finally, we absolutely had to turn in our boarding passes and go. We turned for a last look.

"We love you," Grandpa and Grandma said.

"We love you too," we all said. Justin snapped a picture, and we were gone.

Going *home* is faster than going somewhere. In my opinion. The flight went so fast I hardly had time to think. We had headphones, so Justin and I didn't talk much. During dinner, we talked about the food.

It wasn't until the ride home in our car that I thought about my *real life* again. I started remembering school, and church, and my friends, and the neighborhood, and even Matthew and Mack!

The trees were beautiful. Fall had arrived while we were gone. Everything was a blaze of color—except the grass, which still was green. The closer we got to our home, the more excited I became!

There it was. I think a house really becomes a *home* when you come back to it after a vacation. I carried my suitcase and totes to my room. Wow, it is darling! Before I unpacked, I took a tour through every room. Our furniture and things *belong*. Our books, the pictures, the grape-ivy wreath. I met Mom in the family room. She was walking through the house too. We both smiled.

I forgot to mention *our leaves*. We discovered something we hadn't thought about before. When you live in a woods, the leaves *come down*. Our buttonwood leaves were starting to fall. And we have more than twenty trees in our front yard alone!

"Looks like I'd better get another rake or two," Dad said.

"Or pray for a big wind," I said. Everyone laughed.

"We'll need a million bags," Pete said.

"Too many," Dad said. "Maybe we can haul them into the woods. OK if we get started this afternoon?"

In the end, everybody changed clothes and helped. Pete borrowed three more rakes from Harringtons. Dad got out the wheelbarrow. In an hour, the whole family hadn't made as much as a good start.

"Let's try raking them onto a tarp," Dad suggested. "Then we can drag it down to the woods." He didn't realize how heavy a tarp full of leaves is!

Harringtons drove past on their way to youth group, and waved. And I remembered it was Sunday! It sure didn't seem like it.

When it was getting too dark to rake, we went in our work clothes to the diner for supper. We picked up milk for breakfast on the way home. "Don't forget," Mom reminded, "tomorrow is school."

After supper, it was pitch dark but not very late. I was hanging up my jacket when the phone started to ring. Pete answered, and it was for him.

"Can we get my riding clothes this week?" I asked.

"I don't know anything about them," Mom said. "Why don't you ask Chris to come along with you? Maybe Friday?"

I was just going to dial Chris' number when the phone rang again. I let it ring two more times. No use seeming too anxious. "Hello," I said, "Green residence, Jennifer speaking."

"Hi, Jennifer. It's Lindsay. Have a good time?"

"Great," I said. I didn't think she'd ever call.

"Stephanie and I wondered if you'd like to go to the high-school football game with us Saturday night. Mom will drive."

It was a *miracle*. "I'll have to check. Can you wait while I ask?"

My parents said I could go, so I hurried back to tell her. I started writing things on the calendar.

Chris said she'd be glad to help me pick out my riding clothes. She said she'd check about Friday and let me know. I told her I'd tell her later all about our wonderful time in Florida.

Well, Justin got a call from a *girl,* which had to be Nicole. I couldn't hear what he said to her.

Just as I was unpacking the last of my suitcase, I got another phone call! It was a lady named Mrs. Baldwin. She asked if I could baby-sit for her on Thursday night. I have never baby-sat before. For money, that is. Of course I have stayed with my brothers.

Mom said I could if it wouldn't be too late. I don't know how many kids she has. Mr. Baldwin will pick me up at seven-thirty.

I wrote everything down carefully. It was going to be a *busy week*.

"Remember during the summer when you didn't know anyone?" Mom said. I remembered. Only too well. But that seems so long ago.

17

Busy Week

Lord, it's me, Jennifer.

Even the mornings are dark now. I got dressed Monday morning and headed for the bus stop. It seemed like *everybody* was saying hello to me.

"You look terrific, Jennifer," Stephanie said. I wasn't sure if she was talking about my outfit or my tan.

"Hey, hey. It's Jennifer!" said Matthew. Only he said my name very slowly so it took about half a minute. "We're on the same carnival committee," he said. Probably something to do with Student Council.

I was about to ask him which one, but Mack didn't give me a chance. "We're both on the games committee for the youth group Halloween party," he said.

"Sounds like I'm going to be pretty busy," I said. The bus came.

I saved Heidi's seat. I sure was glad to see her. "They are," I whispered. "My grandparents are Christians," I explained.

Heidi was almost as happy as I am. "Oh, Jennifer, that's just wonderful! We prayed for you in Sunday school. Did you have a good time?"

"It couldn't have been better," I said. "I'll tell you at lunch." With Lindsay and Stephanie sitting behind us, I didn't want to talk.

School was fine. I was afraid I'd be behind, but the homework I had done before I left *did the trick*. I even got an A on my English paper. Although, personally, I don't think it was as good as the first one.

Pete said our family is on a *roll*. He said that means things are going great. Dad told him not to say *roll* anymore. Our biggest problem is the buttonwood leaves. We can't keep up with them. But, as Dad says, we'll figure something out. My brothers and I raked after school.

We were having supper Wednesday night. I remember it very well. We were having meat loaf, and Dad was telling us about the *big contract* his company got while we were in Florida. When the phone rang, he got it himself. "No calls during dinner," he said. "This place is getting to be like a *zoo*."

We didn't pay much attention at first. But when Dad asked, "How are things in Illinois, Bob?" we all got quiet. Our uncle doesn't call much.

"No, I'm not sitting down," Dad said. "Is something wrong?"

I got this terrible feeling in my throat that went down to my stomach.

"Oh, no!" Dad said. We all looked at each other. I held my breath.

"When did you say it happened? ... Do you think I should come too? ..."

I got goose bumps all over. I didn't think I could stand it.

"Of course, I will. Do you have her number handy? I'm not sure we have it.... OK, I have a pencil.... You'll let me know as soon as you know anything.... Yes, Bob. Thanks for calling."

There was absolute silence. Dad came down the three steps into the breakfast room. His face was white. His hand was shaking. His eyes were filling up with tears.

"What is it, dear?" Mom asked softly.

Dad sat down. "It's Pops," he said. "He had a heart attack."

"He'll be OK, won't he?" Pete asked.

"Nobody knows," Dad said. "They took him to the hospital in an ambulance an hour ago. Grandma is at the hospital. The doctors called Uncle Bob. He's going down on the next plane. He doesn't think I should come. He'll call me when there's any news." Dad was breathing deeply, trying to get control of himself. "I have to call Elizabeth."

"Have some coffee first, Peter," Mom said. She got it

for him. Her hands were shaking. "Do you think you should wait until you know more?"

"I don't know, Sue," Dad said.

"What's a heart attack?" Justin wanted to know. "Does it hurt?"

"I think it hurts a lot," Dad said.

I couldn't hold back my tears any longer. They ran down my face.

Dad kept talking, like he was in a daze. "They got him right to the hospital. Fortunately, he wasn't out on the boat. He was just sitting on the balcony of the condo."

I could just picture him there. He loved the view of the canal.

"The first day is the most important," Dad was saying. "If he makes it the first day . . ."

"Does that mean he might die?" Pete asked. I winced. Dad nodded. And then Justin and Mom started crying too.

"It doesn't seem possible," somebody said. I don't know who said it.

"I think I'd better try to call Elizabeth," Dad said. "With the difference in time zones, it may be hard to reach her."

"Where does she live?" I asked.

"Colorado," Dad said. "Near Colorado Springs. I'll call from the study."

He just left us sitting there. We were all crying except Pete. He just kept taking deep breaths. Mom got a box of Kleenex, and we blew our noses.

"Couldn't we pray for him?" Justin said. His face looked so little, his eyes so big.

"Well, sure," I said. "That's exactly what we can do."

Mom looked pretty helpless. I decided we couldn't count on her to be *in charge*. But she stayed with us.

"I'll start," I said. "Unless somebody else wants to." Nobody said anything. "We can take turns." I closed my eyes. "Dear heavenly Father. Thank You for Grandpa and Grandma. Thank You that they both believe in You. Please help Pops to get better."

Pete cleared his throat. "Thank You that he wasn't on the boat when he got sick so he could get to the hospital fast."

"Lord, please help Grandma not to be scared," said Justin.

There was a pause. Mom didn't say anything. I don't think she has ever prayed out loud.

"Please help Dad to call his sister," I said.

"And Uncle Bob to have a safe flight," added Justin.

It was quiet. So I said, "Amen."

Personally, I felt much better. My heart stopped pounding, and the tears were drying up. I could even breathe. "Let's clear the table," I said. Everyone pitched in without complaining.

Mom hugged me. I hugged her back.

Dad came out of his study. "Nobody answers," he said. "The operator is going to try again in half an hour."

"May I call someone now?" I asked.

"OK, but make it short," Dad said.

I wanted to tell somebody in my Sunday-school class, but I couldn't decide which girl. I chose Kelly Robbins, partly because her father is the minister of our church.

"I'm so sorry, Jennifer," Kelly said. "Is it OK if Dad shares it at prayer meeting? The adults meet tonight at seven-thirty."

"Oh, Kelly, that would be wonderful," I said.

"And we'll start the prayer chain for the Sunday-school class," she said. "That way you won't have to call everybody."

"What's a *prayer* chain?" I asked.

"Each girl calls the next one on the list. After she prays, of course," Kelly explained. "You can just call me, and everyone will pray."

"Thank you," I said. "I'll let you know when we hear something. I can't talk any longer now." All of a sudden I felt like crying again.

It was a restless kind of evening. Every time the telephone rang, we all jumped. Reading was impossible. Playing games didn't seem right. We tried to talk, but there wasn't much to say.

Finally, Dad's call got through to Aunt Elizabeth. In Colorado. He took it in the kitchen. We all listened.

"It's Peter, Elizabeth. Yes, your brother.... I'm in Philadelphia. We live here now—since June.... How are you and Steve? ... Well, actually, yes. I have some sad news. Dad had a heart attack in Florida this afternoon.... Are you OK? ... I know. I feel the same way.... Well, fortunately, we just saw them. Last week, in fact.... I know. We can't believe it either.... No, I don't think so. Bob's gone down to be with Mom. He's going to call.... I will let you know.... I've missed you too, Beth.... No, I'll call you either way."

"How is she?" Mom asked.

"OK, I guess," Dad said. "Shocked by the news, of course." Dad drifted off into silence. Pete went over and put his arm around Dad's shoulder. They hugged silently.

The doorbell rang. It hardly ever rings—especially at night.

"I'll get it," Dad said.

"Hi, Peter. Mark Harrington. I heard the news about your father at *prayer meeting*. I just want you to know we're praying. If there's anything we can do, just let us know."

"Thanks," said Dad. "I appreciate it." Mr. Harrington left.

"Do we have to go to school tomorrow?" Justin asked.

"Yes," said Dad, looking at his watch. "Bedtime," he said. His voice was very quiet. And it really wasn't very late. But we went upstairs anyway.

18

Through the Valley

Lord, it's me, Jennifer.

I just can't get to sleep. All I can think about is Grandpa. I know You are busy thinking about him too, Lord. I am glad You can be everywhere at once. Because we need You here too.

Something was rattling around in my head trying to get out. But I absolutely couldn't remember. I tried to pray again, but I couldn't think of anything else to add. Suddenly, as I was thinking about Pops, I remembered something he told me in the car on the way to the airport.

I switched on the light. It was a verse. Then I remembered. I had written down the number on a piece of paper. I grabbed my purse and started hunting. All I had written was GOOD—Romans 8:28. My *study* Bible was in my bookcase. I tried the index. My hands shook as I turned to page 1674. "Letter of Paul to the Romans."

I found chapter 8, then verse 28. "We know that in everything God works for good with those who love Him, who are called according to his purpose." It was Grandpa's letter to Jennifer.

You want us to know You *are in charge*. And everything will turn out good. Right?

I must have gone to sleep. The next thing I knew, it was morning. And I could hear Dad's voice. I dressed so fast I don't know what I wore.

Dad was talking on the kitchen phone, while Mom stirred the oatmeal. "What did the doctor say? . . . What does that mean? . . . How's Mom? . . . Yes, last night. . . . She sounds good. . . . I'm praying too. . . . Do you have my phone number at the office?" Dad gave it to him.

Pete and Justin must have been awake too. They came down in their pajamas and stood on the cold kitchen floor in their bare feet.

"He made it through the night," Dad said. "Grandma is fine, but she won't leave the hospital. Uncle Bob stayed with her, and they took turns resting. The doctor didn't say much this morning. Uncle Bob will call me at the office if there's any change. He thinks they'll be able to visit Grandpa for five minutes later on."

"Dad," I said, "did you know we prayed he'd get well?"

"Mom told me," Dad said.

"Could you pray with us?" Justin asked.

"Get dressed first," Dad said, and Mom agreed. "If we hurry, we can have breakfast together."

We all ate our oatmeal fast. Which was good, since my bus comes first.

"Do you know the Twenty-third Psalm?" Dad asked us. We all shook our heads *no*. Then an amazing thing happened. Without a Bible or anything, Dad started saying it:

"'The Lord is my shepherd; I shall not want.

He maketh me to lie down in green pastures: he leadeth me beside the still waters.

He restoreth my soul: he leadeth me in the paths of righteousness for his name's sake.

Yea, though I walk through the valley of the shadow of death, I will fear no evil: for thou art with me; thy rod and thy staff, they comfort me.

Thou preparest a table before me in the presence of mine enemies: thou anointest my head with oil; my cup runneth over.

Surely goodness and mercy shall follow me all the days of my life: and I will dwell in the house of the Lord forever.'

"Amen," Dad said. And the rest of us said it too.

For the first time, I had to run for the bus.

"Oh, oh, Jennifer overslept," Stephanie said.

Well, I could hardly tell her that my father was reciting the Twenty-third Psalm from memory! "My grandfather is sick," I said.

"Sorry," said Stephanie. "My grandmother was sick once."

Matthew Harrington came from the back of the bus and sat down next to me. He didn't say anything. He didn't have to. I just knew *he cared*. He stayed until Heidi got on a few minutes later. They looked at each other. Then Matthew returned to his seat, and Heidi sat down. And not one person on the bus said a word.

"I'm sorry," Heidi whispered. "We all love you, Jennifer." My eyes filled up with tears again, right on the school bus.

I can't remember when a day was so long. I just went through the motions of going to classes. I could hear the teachers talking, but I didn't know what they were saying. Sometimes my eyes would fill up with tears. I was afraid I'd have to be excused. But then things would be OK again.

On the way home, Mack Harrington sat next to me when Heidi got off. "Any news?" he asked. I shook my head.

My father's car was in the driveway. I didn't know whether to run or walk slowly. I walked slowly.

Everyone was in the living room. My heart sank. I just knew it was *bad news*. Justin was crying. Pete was staring out the window. Mom was blowing her nose. Dad's eyes were red. He got up and put both his arms around me, as I started sobbing.

"Is Pops really dead?" I said. I needed to hear it from my father.

"Yes, Jennifer," Dad said softly. "He died this afternoon. Uncle Bob called me at work, and I came right home. It was too late to get you out of school."

"I can't believe it," I sobbed. "How can somebody be alive and joking and fishing and talking to you one minute and be gone the next week?" Dad didn't say anything. He just held me. My tears fell on his shirt.

"It isn't fair!" I cried. "What did Pops ever do to deserve this?"

Dad's eyes had tears in them too. "Nothing," he said. He held me even tighter.

Well, finally I couldn't cry anymore. I felt weak. I needed to sit down. Mom handed me a Kleenex. Once again I was aware of the rest of my family. Justin's eyes were all red too. And Pete was biting his lower lip.

"We haven't made all the plans yet," Dad said. "But I want you all to know what we've decided so far. Later, I'll be telling you more. And, if you have any questions, just ask me."

We all waited. Dad's voice was gentle. "When someone dies, there is usually a special service to honor him. It's called a *funeral*. Before the service, the family spends some time at a public place called a *funeral home*. Friends can come to comfort the family and honor the one who died."

We have never gone to a *funeral* before. "Where is this going to happen?" I asked.

"In Illinois," Dad said. "My secretary is making our airline reservations now. We'll be going in the morning.

102

Uncle Bob and Grandma will fly up from Florida. We'll all be staying at Uncle Bob's and Aunt Carol's until Monday afternoon."

"So we'll miss more school?" Pete asked.

"That's right," Mom said. "Naturally, any other plans you had for the weekend must be canceled." She looked at me. "Try to make your own calls," she said. "But if you can't do it, I'll help. Also, start laying out clothes to be packed. You'll need dress up things. Not jeans."

It was good to have *something to do*. If I concentrated hard on one thing at a time, I didn't have to *think* or *feel bad*.

After I called Kelly and everyone else, I went to my room. Each time I told somebody else, two things happened. I felt like crying. And it seemed more real. But now it was closing in on me, and I had to get away.

I folded my underwear very carefully. I looked at each dress critically. But I couldn't make any decisions.

There was a knock on my door. It was Pete.

"Come on in," I said. He did, but he just stood there.

"It's OK to cry," I said.

"I know," said my brother. "But what do you do if you can't?" I really didn't know the answer.

Dad finally reached Aunt Elizabeth and told her. She plans to come to Illinois!

Brother Robbins, the minister, called Dad. He offered to come over. Dad said no. Maybe when we get home.

I cried myself to sleep. You might call this working out good, Lord. Personally, I disagree.

19

Back to Illinois

Lord, it's me, Jennifer.

Well, my first visit back to Illinois certainly wasn't anything like I had thought it would be. In the first place, Illinois isn't home anymore. I know that now. In the second place, I was so involved with my family that I hardly got to see any of my friends.

Mr. Harrington took us to the airport. By now we are so used to flying, we just automatically fasten our seat belts. I sat by Dad in a window seat. But it was so rainy and overcast, I could hardly see out the window. The weather matched how I felt.

"Will the sadness ever go away?" I asked.

"It will take time," Dad said.

The takeoff was smooth, but the pilot said we would hit bad weather. That means a bumpy ride and keeping the seat belts on. I wasn't afraid. I didn't even care.

Soon the plane climbed above the clouds. The sunshine was so bright it almost blinded us. The clouds were puffy white. And the view almost took your breath away.

"Dad," I said. "I thought the sun wasn't shining, but it was shining all the time. I just couldn't see it." I looked at him. "Is sadness like that?"

"Jennifer," Dad smiled, "you have more than a writer's ability. You have the heart of a poet."

I felt embarrassed. "One of my teachers says I'm good at analogies," I said.

Aunt Carol met us at the airport. She said Uncle Bob and Grandma had come in earlier. Everyone was waiting for us so they could eat lunch.

"We'll take Mom to the funeral home at two-thirty to make arrangements," Uncle Bob told Dad. "Do you have any idea when Elizabeth arrives?" Dad didn't.

I looked across at Grandma. She seemed almost happy. "He went peacefully," she said. "Just imagine. Now he's with the Lord!"

"Are you sure?" I said.

"Absent from the body, present with the Lord," Grandma repeated. "That's what the Bible says." Then it was like she just realized we were there. "Hello, darlings," she said. "I didn't think I'd be seeing you so soon."

Justin got a funny grin on his face.

"What were you thinking, Justin?" Grandma asked him.

"That's probably what Pops said to the Lord!" Everyone started to laugh.

"Right on!" said Uncle Bob. "That sounds just like him!"

"He had the best sense of humor of anyone I ever knew," Dad said.

"He made everything we ever did fun," said Grandma. Suddenly, tears filled her eyes. "I miss him so much already," she said. And then we all got tears in our eyes. I glanced at Pete. Poor Pete!

That's the way the day went. One minute we were remembering or laughing, the next minute somebody was crying.

I had a couple of minutes to talk to my cousin Sarah, while our fathers were gone with Grandma. "I love Philadelphia," I said. "There's so much to describe and tell you. I don't know where to begin. Do you think you can come for a visit?"

"I hope so," Sarah said. The biggest thing in her life right now is a boy named Scott. "He goes to our church, so maybe you'll see him," she said.

Well, I told her about the Harrington brothers, and my horseback riding, and church. I ended up with *youth group* and the *retreat*. "I'm not very good at talking about Him," I said, "but I do believe in Jesus." Sarah said she was glad. But then she started talking about Scott again.

♦ ♦ ♦ ♦

"Well, now we just have to meet with the minister," Uncle Bob said to Grandma when they got home. "Why don't you lie down and try to sleep?"

Grandma did look tired. "I'll try," she said. "Where do you want me to nap?" The sleeping situation was a real problem. It was solved mainly by putting most of the cousins in sleeping bags in the rec room. But it was nice to be together. Mom's mother, Grandma Andrews, thought we should come over to their house, but Dad said *no thanks*.

Dad had promised to let us know about the plans, and he remembered. "The *visitation* at the *funeral home* will be Sunday from three to nine," he told us and our cousins. "The entire family will go over early at two-thirty for a private time before people come. The *funeral* service will be Monday morning at ten o'clock at the church."

"Can we visit our friends tomorrow?" Pete asked.

"I'll take you over to our old neighborhood sometime," Dad said.

I tried to call three friends before I realized they were still in school! Somehow it seems as if *everything should stop* during a crisis. But it doesn't. It just runs in *slow motion*.

I was trying to decide which was more painful—thinking or just sitting around. Thinking won. I was just sitting on a couch when I heard some activity. In fact, *noise*.

With a flurry of excitement and a falling-off muffler,

Aunt Elizabeth arrived. She had driven all the way from Colorado by herself.

"Peter!" she said, throwing her arms around my father. "Where's Mom? And Bob?"

"I didn't know you were driving, Beth," Dad said.

"I go by Elizabeth, brother dear," she said. "If I had told you, you'd have insisted I fly. And, frankly, we don't have the money. Where's the bathroom?"

She has long, brown hair and a face like Mary Poppins. And, all of a sudden, the house was alive again.

Naturally, Grandma hurried down. "Elizabeth! Elizabeth, dear," she said, hugging her daughter.

"I can't believe it about Dad," Aunt Elizabeth said. "Was he sick at all?"

"Less than a day," Grandma said. "For him, it was a beautiful way to go."

"Was he awake?" she asked.

"Yes, sometimes," Grandma said. "I was with him at the end." All of us were listening to every word. I'm not sure it was too respectful, but we all were curious.

"Did I tell you what he said?" asked Grandma.

Well, she must have forgotten, for no one knew.

"He said, 'Tell Elizabeth I love her,'" Grandma repeated. That made Aunt Elizabeth cry.

But Grandma wasn't finished. "Then he said he'll be waiting for me." She sort of had a faraway look on her face. Not sad. More expectant. Everyone in the room was very quiet. Suddenly, Grandma remembered something else. "He said, 'Give Pete my fishing hat!'"

I looked at my brother. Tears were streaming down his face, and he was trembling. Everybody in the family was crying. Including me. Dad edged over to Pete, and they stood together sobbing.

We didn't notice when Grandma left, but all of a sudden she was back, handing the famous cap to Pete.

"Think you're up to the *responsibility,* Son?" Dad asked.

"Pops must have thought so," Pete said. He put the hat on his head and left it there. Mom didn't say a word.

Well, naturally the wave of sadness passed, and pretty soon everyone was telling fish stories. Then Dad and Uncle Bob and Aunt Elizabeth were remembering the past. We were fascinated.

"Remember the time I bought Dad three laundry-marking pens for Christmas?" Dad said. "I didn't know for years they weren't ballpoint pens!"

"Remember the time I brought the frog in, and I got scared, and it got away?" said Uncle Bob.

"Did you get spanked?" Grandma asked. "I can't recall."

"I can't either," said Uncle Bob, "but I hid in Beth's room for hours."

Personally, I can't imagine Uncle Bob being naughty. Or Dad. Well, maybe Aunt Elizabeth!

When we were so exhausted we were dozing off anyway, the kids were sent to bed. As I lay in my sleeping bag, I could hear talking and laughing. The crying was too quiet to hear.

20

We Say Good-bye

Lord, it's me, Jennifer.

Since for Saturday there were no special plans, it just sort of happened as we went along. And when it didn't happen, Aunt Elizabeth filled in. We woke up on the rec room floor to find her with us. Her nice down sleeping bag was mended with a piece of bright orange tape.

"Hi, everybody," she said. At first nobody knew what to say to her. But by breakfast we felt we had a new friend. She called it "getting to know her nieces and nephews." She asked *good questions* that made us think. "What did you enjoy most about your grandfather?" Stuff like that.

After breakfast, Grandma and Grandpa Andrews

came over. If Mom's mother is still upset because we moved, she didn't show it. "I want to hear all about Pennsylvania," she said. But when we'd start to tell her something, she'd always interrupt and start talking about herself.

As more of our parents' friends dropped in, Aunt Elizabeth worked out a big 7-Up Game downstairs. She is just like Grandma, only even peppier. We couldn't be loud, but we did have fun.

After lunch, Dad and Mom took us back to our old neighborhood.

"The houses look so small and close together," Pete said.

"I feel like I've been gone for years," said Mom. "Oh, look! They've taken down our living-room curtains." We drove past our house slowly, noticing all the changes. It may still be called the *old Green house,* but it didn't seem like home to us any longer. We all agreed on that.

"Anybody special you want to see?" Dad asked.

For Pete it was pretty easy. He had only had one friend in Illinois. Pete and Joseph both liked books better than sports. And for good reason, I might add. We stopped in front of Joseph's house. Pete ran up to the door and soon came back to ask if he could stay half an hour.

Justin had had so many friends that it was hard for him to choose. Finally, Dad stopped at Tony's. Turned out everybody was at soccer practice, so we dropped him off there.

My friend Laurie was at the orthodontist. Susan had a

piano lesson. Nobody at all was home at Beth's. I thought everybody would be just waiting to see me. Maybe I should have called. Still, their lives were going on without me.

I felt very *let down*. I had lost my grandpa and all my old friends in three days.

Dad swung by to get Pete. He already was standing outside waiting. I couldn't believe it.

"Anything wrong?" Dad asked.

"No. He's really into science fiction and computers," Pete said. "I'm not."

"We'll probably have a hard time getting Justin to leave," Dad predicted.

Wrong. He was waiting for us too. "Everybody glad to see you?" Dad wondered.

"I guess so," said Justin. "They all said hi." Then he nearly knocked our socks off. "They weren't really very meaningful relationships," he said.

When we got back, Aunt Elizabeth had worked out a Ping-Pong tournament that sounded pretty good. Uncle Bob's home seemed warm and safe. Why had I always thought *family* was so boring? I can't remember.

Sunday morning everybody went together to Uncle Bob's church. It had been Grandma and Pops' church also. That's where the *funeral* service would be held. Personally, I would have enjoyed going back to my old Sunday-school class, but I had *no choice*.

Some ladies called Deaconesses brought our dinner to Aunt Carol's. We had real meat. And homemade pies. I think Deaconess must mean good cook. Afterwards, we had to stay in our church clothes, since we were going to the funeral home at two-thirty.

"I said I'd explain what would be happening," Dad said, as he gathered us kids together in the family room.

"Our whole family will be together in a large room, like a living room, only bigger," Dad explained. "There will be lots of flower arrangements. Somewhere in the room will be a long sort of box, called a casket. Inside will be Grandpa's body."

Nobody said anything. I put my hand on Justin's shoulder. I felt very calm, so why was my hand shaking?

"Your grandfather," Dad said, as his eyes filled with tears, "is with Jesus, in Heaven. We will be sort of saying 'good-bye' to the part of Pops that we could see." Dad blew his nose. "Don't feel anything is expected of you. If you'd rather just remember him as you knew him, that's OK."

Dad looked to see if we were all right. "We'll be in the room together until three o'clock. After that, we expect many friends to come, stay a while, and then leave. They loved Grandpa too, and they want to show us they care— for him and for us."

"Is it OK to cry?" Pete asked.

"It is," Dad said. "Some of the friends may cry also. We will miss him, and that is sad. But Pops will live forever in Heaven. So we aren't as sad as we would be if we didn't believe in Jesus."

"Will it be sort of like at Uncle Bob's?" I asked.

"Some crying, and some remembering, and maybe even laughing sometimes?"

"Exactly, Jennifer. We will be expressing lots of different emotions at different times. You can't always control how you'll feel." Dad looked at his watch. "We'd better put our coats on. It's time to leave."

Even the weather was like our feelings—kind of mixed-up. It wasn't really raining. But the mist was so heavy we needed our windshield wipers on. I remembered that above the clouds the sun is shining.

When we got there, the *funeral home* was very quiet. A man in a black suit hung up our coats.

"Mom, over here," Dad said to Grandma. He was clearly *in charge*. Maybe because he is the oldest. He took Grandma's hand. "OK, everyone," he said, "join hands in a circle." We did.

"Before we go in, we're going to pray." I could hardly believe it. But that's just what we did. "Our dear heavenly Father," Dad said, "be with us now. Bless us and the friends who come. Help the children not to be afraid. Thank You that Dad isn't sick now. We hope You enjoy him as much as we did. Amen."

I felt really connected to everyone in the circle. I love our family!

The man in the black suit opened the double doors. It was just as Dad had described it.

"Let's wait for Grandma," Dad said. "Do you want one of us to go with you?"

"I'll be OK, Peter," she said. She walked slowly to the

114

casket. She looked small somehow. She stood there looking at Pops. She dried her wet cheeks. Then she turned
toward the rest of us. She looked like a bride, only older.

The rest of us went in together. It wasn't scary or aw-
ful. In some ways it looked like Pops, but it wasn't hard
to believe he is really in Heaven. He's never been that
still. And he was wearing a navy blue coat, a white shirt,
and a tie. His hands held his well-worn Bible.

Gradually I was aware of the rest of the family. Some
were wiping tears from their eyes. And there was lots of
hugging. Dad had his arm around Aunt Carol's shoulder.
Pete was with Mom. Sarah and Michael were with Uncle
Bob. And there, beside me, was Justin. Aunt Elizabeth
stood next to her father for a long time.

And then the friends started coming. Sometimes there
were so many at once that they had to stand in line.
During other times the adults walked around, or sat on a
sofa, or went to a little room for coffee.

"I'm so sorry," said a woman to my father. "Your dad
sold us our first bedroom furniture. We still have it."

"Thanks for coming," Dad said. He said that a lot.

There were reunions of people who hadn't seen each
other for a long time. And some laughing. I think
Grandpa would have liked that.

The flowers. Did I mention the flowers? They were
something else—like a garden in the summertime. A big
blanket of yellow roses on the bottom part of the casket
had letters that spelled out "Husband" and "Father."
And a little matching bouquet said "Grandpa."

"Jennifer." I was surprised to hear my name. It was my old Sunday-school class!

I started to cry. "Thank you for coming," I said. Everyone crowded around me and hugged me.

My father was standing nearby, and he came over to meet them. "I'm sure your Grandma would like to meet your friends," Dad suggested.

"He was such a wonderful husband," Grandma told the girls. "I will miss him so much. We were married thirty-nine years. Now he's with Jesus, waiting for me." She didn't cry that time, but two of my friends did.

Dad suggested I take the class into the coffee room so we could talk better. I discovered I haven't lost all my friends in Illinois. I told them about my Sunday-school class and *youth group*. And I told them about the *retreat* where I became a Christian. They were so happy!

"Remember when I first came to Sunday school?" I asked. "And I thought God's name was Hallowed B.?"

"That was just last year, wasn't it? I can't believe it," said my teacher. Neither can I.

Finally all the friends were gone. We were back down to our family and two men in black suits. We sort of took turns saying "good-bye" to Pops. I went up with my brothers. We stood there with our arms around each other. I heard someone join us. It was Mom and Dad.

"Aren't you glad we really got to say good-bye last week?" I said. Dad nodded, tears streaming down his cheeks.

It was time to go home.

21

What Pops Believed

Lord, it's me, Jennifer.

The *funeral* service was a lot like church. Our whole family came in together right before it started. We sat in the front row. Grandpa's casket was in the front, all closed up. The rosebuds had opened, and it was beautiful.

When we stood up to sing, "All the Way My Savior Leads Me," I could hear lots of people singing the beautiful words of faith.

"Let us listen to the Word of God," said the minister.

"Jesus said: 'Do not let your hearts be troubled. Trust in God; trust also in me. In my Father's house are many rooms; if it were not so, I would have told you. I am going there to prepare a place for you.' (John 14:1, 3)

'Now we know that if the earthly tent we live in is destroyed, we have a building from God, an eternal house in heaven, not built by human hands.'" (2 Corinthians 5:1)

Next a man sang "The Lord Is My Shepherd." I remembered the words from when my father recited Psalm 23 the morning Grandpa went to Heaven.

I glanced down the row. Grandma's face wore an expression of *peace*. And no one else was crying either. Everybody was listening carefully to the minister.

"My dear friends, Jay Green was a man of strong faith. When the Lord said something, Jay believed it. Dear Mary Green, gave me the privilege of looking through her husband's Bible. It was underlined with Jay's pen. And many times, next to a verse, Jay Green had written a simple *yes*.

"Today I want to share with you—his wife, his children, his grandchildren, and his many friends—one underlined verse, John 11:25. I will read it from a newer translation so the grandchildren can better understand the meaning.

"Jesus' friend Lazarus had died. Jesus was so sad that the Bible tells us He wept. But, in talking to the dead man's sister Martha, Jesus said this:

'I am the resurrection and the life. He who believes in me will live, even though he dies; and whoever lives and believes in me will never die. Do you believe this?' (John 11:25)

"Justin Templeton Green had underlined this verse. And, as if to answer Jesus' question himself, Jay had written *yes*.

"We can say, with certainty, that when it was Jay Green's turn to meet the Lord, he did so with belief.

"There will be days of sadness and loneliness. But let none of you leave this service with any doubt that Jay Green is in Heaven."

After the minister prayed, everybody stood and sang "Blessed assurance, Jesus is mine! Oh, what a foretaste of glory divine!" It was like a *heavenly choir*.

Then the men in black suits wheeled the casket out. Some men carried it to a big black car, like a station wagon only longer. Our family followed and got into big white cars. Grandma, Uncle Bob, Aunt Elizabeth, and Dad rode together—they were Grandpa's own family.

A whole string of cars drove behind in the procession. Each one had a purple flag on the antenna and drove with its lights on. We went right through stop signs!

The cemetery is on the edge of town. And it is beautiful! One tree was so red it could have been on a magazine. And others were pure gold in the sunshine.

I guess I never thought about where my grandparents would be buried. But they had it planned all along. The men carried Grandpa's casket to a spot under a golden tree. I could tell somebody had dug a hole, although they put fake grass around it.

There were a few folding chairs set up under a sort of tent. Aunt Elizabeth sat down with Grandma. The rest of us crowded around.

The minister cleared his throat. "Psalm 16:11 assures us of the future ahead for believers. 'Thou dost show me the path of life; in thy presence there is fullness of joy, in thy right hand are pleasures for evermore.'

"With the apostle Paul, Jay Green has said, 'I have finished the race, I have kept the faith.'" (2 Timothy 4:7)

After the prayer, I was surprised to hear a weak voice start to sing. "When we all get to heaven, what a day of rejoicing that will be!" It was Grandma. All the people standing around joined in and sang with her.

Now the tears were running down my face again. But they were tears of joy.

◆ ◆ ◆ ◆

Aunt Elizabeth left after lunch. She invited us to come to see them in Colorado. And we invited them to visit us.

Grandma Green will stay on a while with Uncle Bob's family. I hated to leave, but naturally we can't miss any more school. And Dad has to go back to work.

We said our good-byes at Uncle Bob's. I think it was harder than when we moved! To leave all this love and support was sadness again.

I sat with Justin on the plane. "Are you OK?" I asked.

"There's only one thing I don't understand," he said. I wondered if it was the same thing that's bothering me.

"What's that?" I asked.

"If Dad really believes, how come we never knew it before?"

My problem exactly. "I don't know, Justin. I think we'll just have to ask him."

I had to wait for the right time. It took a little while.

Mr. Harrington was at the airport to meet us. "Thanks for coming, Mark," Dad said.

"Everything go all right?" Mr. Harrington asked. "How's your mom doing?"

"Fine," Dad said.

It was dark outside. I couldn't see the beautiful *welcome home* from the hills and trees. Mostly we didn't talk. Justin and Mom fell asleep right in the car. Pete, wearing Pops' fishing hat, stood out against the lights.

But, when we pulled into our lane, the headlights lit up a green lawn!

"The leaves," I said. "What happened to the leaves?"

Mr. Harrington spoke softly. "It was one thing the Harringtons could do," he said.

When we got inside Dad clasped Mr. Harrington's hand warmly. "Mark, how can I ever thank you? You'll never know how much we need to feel love here!"

It was only the beginning. When Mom went into the kitchen, she found milk in the refrigerator. And on the counter by the phone was a list of people from our church who would be bringing supper over every night during the coming week. Mom got tears in her eyes.

We were home.

22

Another Family

Lord, it's me, Jennifer.

The kids and teachers at school all knew. I could tell. Some kids avoided me entirely. Others seemed to feel they should say something, but they didn't know what. I could sort of tell who had experience and who didn't.

The simplest comments were the easiest for me to handle. Stuff like "I'm sorry." Or "I care." Or "I understand." Usually I smiled and said "Thank you." I knew that nobody would say the wrong thing on purpose.

I felt numb but peaceful. I also felt hopelessly behind in my classes, but my teachers assured me I'd be able to catch up. Pete, Justin, and I used our spare time on homework. It's the only time I can ever remember us all spending time together after school and after supper studying. We seemed to want to be together. Mom let us sit around the family room table.

Dad had lots of catching up to do at work. But on Wednesday night he brought work home and joined us. We had to put another leaf in the table.

About 9 P.M. the phone rang. "It's for you, Dad," Justin said. "It's the minister, Brother Robbins."

"He's coming over tomorrow evening," Dad said. I realized the only time Dad had seen him was when he pitched at the church softball game.

♦ ♦ ♦ ♦

Brother Robbins was right on time. "Just call me Stephen," he said to Dad and Mom.

"We're Peter and Sue Green," Dad said. "I guess you know our children?"

Brother Robbins smiled. "Yes," he said, "they're a fine addition to our church young people."

While we were sitting down in the living room, Mom thanked him for the meals the church families were bringing over.

"Well," said Brother Robbins, "we just want you to know that we care about you. We are ready to do anything we can to help." He paused, and nobody else said anything. "You just visited your parents in Florida, didn't you?"

"Yes," Dad said. "Thank goodness. In some ways

that's made it harder, because it doesn't seem possible. But we are so glad we went."

"You've had a lot of traveling. I'll bet you must be tired."

Mom was relaxing more. "Yes, but now it is hard to be alone again and back to a normal routine." I was surprised. Mom doesn't talk much about how she feels.

"We know we can't replace your family," Brother Robbins said, "but we do have a warm church family. I'd like to invite you to visit and meet us."

"They already know the Harringtons," Pete said.

"That's a good start," the minister smiled. "A wonderful family!"

We all agreed.

"I just thought you might have questions on your minds," Brother Robbins said. "Was this the first funeral you young people went to?" We all nodded.

"The minister in Illinois said Grandpa is in Heaven," said Justin. "Because he believed and had accepted Jesus as his Savior." He glanced at Dad.

"That's wonderful news," Brother Robbins said.

"Does Pops know what we're doing? Can he see us?" Pete asked.

"Pops must be what you called your grandfather," Brother Robbins said. "The Bible seems to teach that there is no direct communication between the living and those who have gone on ahead to Heaven. But we can feel very close to our loved ones anyway. Of course, we remember them. But also we know that your grandpa is worshiping Jesus right now. When we worship, we're joining those already in Heaven."

"I never thought about that," Dad said.

"When we get to Heaven, will we know each other?" I wanted to know.

"I'm sure we will," Brother Robbins said. "When Jesus came back from the grave, His friends knew Him."

"Grandpa loved to fish," Pete said. "Can he fish in Heaven?"

Brother Robbins smiled. "We'll have to wait and see. There's lots about Heaven we don't know."

Justin was grinning like a ninny. I hoped he wasn't going to say something stupid. "Is Pops an angel?" he asked.

All of a sudden I got this mental picture of Pops sitting on a cloud with wings and a halo and a harp! I started laughing, and everyone else joined in, even Dad.

Brother Robbins laughed too. "Well," he said, "In the first place, we aren't sure what angels really look like. We have no pictures of them except what artists have made up. But, in the second place, people and angels aren't the same kind of beings."

Mom offered to make some coffee, but Brother Robbins said he couldn't stay. "If you need me for anything at all," he said, "please let me know." He prayed before he left.

"Seems like a fine man," Dad commented.

"And he does have a good fastball," Justin remembered.

"Dad," I said, "could I talk with you alone for a minute?"

"Sure," he said. "Let's go into the study."

"I'm confused about something," I said.

"Why didn't you ask Brother Robbins?"

"Because it doesn't concern him," I said.

"Sounds serious," Dad said. We both sat down. "OK, I'm ready."

"Well," I said, "I don't understand why you've never gone to church or anything all my life. And why you never took us kids until last year. And now, no offense, but all of a sudden you act like you believe. I just don't get it."

"I'm not very proud of my reasons, Jennifer. But try to understand." He looked like it mattered a lot to him. I nodded. "As you realize, I grew up in a Christian home. I learned to pray almost before I could talk. We almost lived at the church—never missed anything. At Sunday school I memorized Bible verses. Even won awards for attendance and memorizing."

"But did you understand what it meant to be a Christian?" I asked.

Dad looked sad. "Yes. I accepted Jesus and was baptized when I was in my teens."

I was more and more confused.

"But then I rebelled. I didn't want to work in the furniture store. I didn't want to go to a Christian college. Not that either of those things really matter. But it was easy to go along with the crowd at the university. It was easy to sleep in on Sunday. And I just got to where the Lord didn't seem part of my life anymore."

"How about Mom?" I asked.

"She never did go to church. So when we got married, it wasn't part of our habits. I can't blame her, because she didn't know any difference. But I felt so guilty about you kids I could hardly stand it sometimes."

"Gosh," I said, "I never realized that."

"It just shows you that the Lord is greater than we realize. I know He wanted you to hear the *truth*. And He bypassed me and my stubbornness to show you His love."

"When did you start realizing what you were doing?" I wondered. "When Grandpa died?"

"No, before that. I think when we moved out here and were so alone. Our money couldn't buy the things we really needed—friendship, love, even faith. And I could see how meaningful the Lord was becoming in your life."

"Dad," I said, "do you believe in Jesus now?"

"Yes, Jennifer. I do. I was just too proud to admit I needed Him." He looked at me. "Do you?" he asked.

"Since the *retreat*," I said.

"Praise the Lord," he said softly. I thought I would faint.

♦ ♦ ♦ ♦

On Sunday morning my brothers and I went to Sunday school, as usual, with the Harringtons. We were meeting before church, when Matthew spotted Dad and Mom. He and I walked over.

"Welcome," Matthew said. "Would you like to sit with us?"

My parents seemed happy. "Sounds good," Dad said. As we walked, he leaned down and whispered something to me. "It's a start," he said, smiling.

Well, we couldn't fit both families into one row, so our family ended up sitting behind the Harringtons. I tried to concentrate on the service, but it was hard. Once, when we were listening to the choir, my eye caught the back of a white-haired man. It looked like Pops! I could hardly breathe for a second. Naturally, it was somebody else.

Later, during the sermon, I glanced down our row. First me, then Pete, Dad, Justin, and Mom. All together, as a family, in Your house, Lord. It felt peaceful. And *right*. Our grandpa would have been happy. I guess I have to admit that maybe Pops was right. Things are turning out for *good* after all.